Emily's Seams

J.E. Flanagan

For Aaron

Chapters

Prologue

The casket was white. The flowers were pink and white. My decrepit aunt, Jude, had picked everything, even the black dress and nylons I was wearing. I guess she thought that I would have been too upset to do any of this myself. True, I don't know who would have done it if she hadn't, but it's not because I was too sad. I didn't care. Julia was gone. Did it really matter what colour the flowers were or how shiny of a box we put her in?

When I was younger I used to daydream that I had super powers. Something about me had to be special and I convinced myself whatever this hidden talent of mine was, it would show itself when the time was right. Just when my special gifts were needed the most. Of course most people dream about this at some point in their life. We can't watch hours and hours of television shows and movies about the only one who could save us all not to imagine, not to hope, that maybe that would be us someday. We would be that special one in a million to be loved for how important and unique and amazing we were. Of course, we all get older and this fantasy dissipates but it does not disappear. Instead, our super powers morph into things like being the most beautiful, the highest paid, the best. For me, this natural progression happened just as expected, but there was always a tinge of that childhood hope leftover. I wanted to be able to fly or speak with animals. Maybe I could move things with my mind or I could see the future. Some kind of special above that of most.

But as they lowered her into the dark ground for a cold and lonely eternity the surprisingly brutal truth that I was not special finally set in. Because if I had been, even just a little, I would have been able to save her.

1

Stranger

I knew he was there. I could hear him breathing through his mouth and shuffling his feet. I didn't look up at him. Instead, I quickly glanced at his feet. His pants were too long. I wondered how much dust he was now dragging around.

"Em?"

I still didn't look up. "Emily."

"Sorry. Right, I forgot you hate it when people shorten your name." he said shyly.

"No, Robert, you're wrong. I hate it when people shorten anyone's name. I think it makes them sound stupid and lazy." I still didn't look up at him. Looking through the microscope I could see that the cells were almost confluent. Maybe one more day to go.

"Oh." He waited. His feet shuffled.

I still didn't look up.

"I'm leaving now and wanted to see if you were up for getting some dinner." he said quickly. "There's a little sushi place around the corner and they have amazing California rolls." he added.

Oh yes. California rolls would be the deciding factor here.

"No." My pace at the microscope was slowing. He was slowing me down.

"Okay. Maybe some other time?" He didn't sound hopeful.

"Probably not." I replied.

"Emily?"

I sighed. "What?"

His feet shuffled again, like he was trying to stand up a little taller. "You're kind of...well, mean." His voice didn't quite carry the tone that I'm sure he'd hoped standing up straight might convey.

"Yeah. You're probably right." One more flask of cells to look at.

He shuffled away. I still didn't look up. I already knew what I'd see. Slumped shoulders underneath a ratty white lab coat, covered in staining supplies.

It had been a shit day at the lab. It was dull. It was boring. I couldn't wait to leave except that I really had nowhere to go. My aunt Jude would be home, puffing away in her recliner, watching whatever was on the television.

It's made of real leather, she'd say as she smoothed her crumpled hand over the dark green skin of her chair.

No, I couldn't go home. Not yet.

As I stepped out of the building, the fresh air hit me like a bucket of ice water. It was so beautiful out. I turned the opposite direction from my house and started walking.

The rows of non-descript houses seemed to end abruptly, as if they had finally given up on trying to get my attention. I walked through a park and into the industrial crypt of town. There was no longer a truck-making industry here. It died out when the selling price got too good for the local owners to stand their ground. Can't say I blame them. I heard they moved to Phoenix with all that cash. The city as a whole didn't seem to notice, but this one neighbourhood did. The business was shut down and the buildings were left to rot. I passed through this part of town as quickly as possible.

Suddenly I was standing at the end of a street, staring at a wall of trees. There was a worn foot path like an old scar in the forest's underbrush.

The clouds had fattened and darkened, telling me it was time to head back. But I just couldn't. Not today. The trail was littered with banana peels and water bottles but it was easy to follow. At one point the trail forked. One branch headed up and the other down.

I went down.

I could hear the patter of the rain on the forest canopy overhead. It was a nice sound. I didn't know what to expect but I was surprised to see the forest thin and then disappear completely.

In the center of the forest clearing was a building. It was two stories, made of brick and looked like it had been empty for years. As I stood there staring at it, the rain began to fall harder and faster. I was getting soaked. I ran towards the old building and passed through the open front doors under an awning with rusted letters.

Creekside Institute.

I had heard stories about this place as a kid. This was where crazy people were stashed. Someone was murdered here. They hid aliens in the basement. The usual.

The walls inside the forgotten hospital were covered in graffiti and not the kind you could almost appreciate. Oddly shaped penises and poorly drawn women with swollen genitalia looked back at me as I took a few steps down the hall. The childish drawings were accompanied by beer cans, condoms and empty chip bags.

Yes, this was a place of healing. Sexual, juvenile, drunken healing.

The place smelled so stale that I knew no one else had been inside for awhile. The old smell of piss still lingered in the air but the musk of the mould and mildew that was probably filling my lungs with toxic spores was stronger.

I turned right at the end of the hall and headed down the next corridor to get a look outside from the window. I couldn't believe the glass was still intact. I pulled myself up by the metal grate that covered the window and looked out onto the sorriest excuse of a garden ever. An empty plot would have looked nicer than the dead foliage twisted around old, wooden posts. A picnic table of rotting wood stood by like a set of forgotten bleachers. No one cheered on the little garden anymore. This particular home team had disappointed just one too many times.

I seriously doubted that any real push for recovery had gone on at this hospital. Even in its heyday, it still would have been a shit hole.

A squeak down at the opposite end of the hall made me turn from the window. I hadn't heard the main door open after I had come inside but suddenly I knew I wasn't alone. And it wasn't just the sound. I could see delicate twists of cigarette smoke wafting out of one of the rooms.

I didn't get nervous that often. Probably because I didn't care about most things anymore. But I can't lie, my heart was going a little faster. I quietly made my way to where the hall turned back to the entrance and thought about making a run for the door. There was probably some sex depraved homeless meth addict in that room.

But I didn't leave. Instead, the dumber Emily, the one with no thoughts of self-preservation, picked up my feet and walked me to the room. I didn't know what to expect, but it was not this.

An old man, maybe in his seventies, was sitting on a plucked and stained mattress in the middle of the room. He looked at me, but didn't say anything. Instead, he just raised his bony hand to his face and sucked on his cigarette like it was the best thing he'd ever tasted.

I realized then that Dumb Emily had kind of wanted to see something grotesque. The rest of me though was relieved.

"Crazy weather, eh?" I said.

He looked at me now like he actually saw me for the first time. He didn't say anything, he just nodded once.

"Okay." I raised my hand in a stiff, awkward wave and turned to leave.

"Wait." he croaked.

I thought about leaving anyways but then decided against it. Any old man in a weathered Red Sox cap and a cigarette pack tucked into the sleeve of his rolled up t-shirt deserved a second or two.

"You with the black hair. Can you see me?"

I'm sure my face twisted with that *what the fuck are you talking about* look but I still nodded.

"Wow." That was all he said for an entire minute. I know that doesn't seem long but his cigarette was burning down quickly and getting dangerously close to his fingers. And I was just standing there.

"What year is it?" he asked.

I didn't think he was stupid for asking. If someone didn't know what year it was, it's probably because they'd been in a coma, avoiding the actually stupid people in their life for as long as possible.

"It's twenty-eleven."

His eyes were unequally framed by saggy, wrinkled skin. They opened a little wider as he nodded in appreciation of what I had just said. "Well then..."

He took another long and satisfying drag of his near spent cigarette and stood up slowly. Not because he was old but because he was just that cool.

There wasn't much left of his cigarette but he gently brushed the lit end of the butt until it was out and then carefully tucked the remnants away in the cigarette pack in his other hand.

"My name's Angus. I've got to get back to my friends now." He suddenly seemed to perk up with a great idea. "Say, you wouldn't want to meet them, would ya?"

"Will there be shuffle board and digestive cookies?"

His eyes brightened a little and he smiled. "I know, I know. Why hang out with an old gramps like me, right? Well, I wouldn't have asked except that you seem a little alone and we could use a new face. Would probably cheer us up. I guess you could say you'd be doing us a solid." Each word had an ease to it as if it came with a cold beer and a sunny day.

He was tall and thin. I had no trouble picturing Angus in another time when he was young, strong and played with the hearts of young girls like they were dice. Meant for shaking and throwing. He was past that now, that was obvious, but there was something else.

6

I could tell when someone liked me. Or at least how I looked. It was clear I wasn't his type.

"Okay." I could feel Dumb Emily nodding our head.

He smiled. "They're over here." He walked by me and into the hall. I assumed he'd head to the entrance but he didn't. Instead, he ducked into the room beside the one I had found him in. It was another patient room but bigger. It had the skeletons of four single beds, one rusting in each corner of the room.

"Franny doesn't like the smell of my smokes. Makes me leave if I want to smoke them." He looked at the pack of cigarettes in his hand wistfully. "Lucky for her, I'm almost out." He huffed, sort of a non-verbal *oh hell,* and tucked his cigarette pack into the rolled up sleeve of his t-shirt.

"We're through here." I looked at the wall he motioned to. It had cracks reaching down it from where the rain had weakened the ceiling. The paint, that odd toothpaste blue color, was chipped in some places and peeling in others. It was just a crummy, disintegrating wall.

And then the strangest thing happened. The dirty plaster began to peel in on itself. It rolled over the patches of blue paint that had survived the years. The folds of plaster got fatter and fatter until a jagged hole had formed in the wall.

I didn't have to look at Angus to know he was smiling at me.

"Crazy shit, huh?"

I just nodded. With each step my feet pushed some old rubbish out of the way. A crusty newspaper. An old beer can. Candy wrappers. My only witnesses to this *crazy shit.*

I looked into the hole and saw a clean white room on the other side. I looked back at Angus and his smug smile, and then glanced over the room I was actually living and breathing in. It was like the white room's ugly, deformed cousin that was normally kept hidden away in an attic and fed scraps. But this was the room on display for the world. The other one, the white room, was the one being stashed.

"What the fuck is this?" My voice was so small.

Angus sighed. "We think it's purgatory. Too clean to be hell."

I ran.

It was raining even harder when I dashed out of the building but that didn't stop me. The trail that ran up through the forest was slick now and I fell more than once. I shot out of the forest and ran down the street, soaked through. My tights were torn and covered in mud from my multiple falls. I must have looked pretty bad but the few people I passed on my run home didn't say much of anything, just a few sideways glances.

They didn't just see a wall open up in an abandoned crazy house. No. It didn't open up, it melted. I ran it over in my head again and again but it didn't make sense. I'd been in stasis for so long now and this had violently ripped me out of it.

Snip. A seam. Just one. But it was the first one that had failed me since the patch-up job I had done when she left.

After forty minutes in the rain, I was home. My building was an older four story affair, straight from the seventies. Huntsville was full of them. Normally I was fine with it, the lack of a functional elevator didn't get me down, but today I was cold, wet and winded from my run.

The trudge up to the third floor was hell. The adrenaline had exhausted my muscles and my mind. I was slipping into that fatigue that inevitably follows a rush.

My hand shook as I tried to open the door to my apartment. It took me four tries but the key finally found the lock. I warily stepped into my warm and musty home.

I could hear my aunt Jude snoring away in her recliner. I dropped my bag at the door and went through the kitchen and into the living room. Mr. Puggums was sleeping in her lap, snoring just as loudly.

He poked his furry head up as I turned the television off. He meowed at me like an old organ that had been burned and left to rot.

"Shut up, Puggums." I whispered. I patted his scraggly hair and scratched behind his ears. I could see him kneading his paws into my aunt's thigh but I didn't worry about it waking her. A long time ago she'd striped this cat of any dignity. No balls. No claws.

My aunt's jaw hung slack as she snored again. She twisted her skinny body a little in the recliner, farted, and then went right back to snoring. Mr. Puggums didn't seem to mind any of this.

The hot shower finished whatever calming down the forty minute run home in the rain hadn't.

I couldn't believe what I'd seen tonight. It just couldn't be real. I looked at myself in the mirror as if she were another person who was supposed to figure this out.

Nothing.

"Guess we're going back tomorrow then." I said. Pretty sure Dumb Emily had just piped up there but it didn't matter now anyways. I was going to go back. I wanted to see that place again.

Purgatory's Guests

The next day at the lab dragged on. The boss had me book flights for him and his star grad student, Robert, to go to a conference in Atlanta. There were people like travel agents that could do this but the boss liked the idea of an assistant. Asked me to get him coffee on my first day. I considered Tabasco sauce or spit but then I realized I was putting in way too much energy. So I just didn't. He asked me again every morning for a week before finally giving in to my noncompliance.

But I was bored today. There was too little to do but I needed to be there until the slides I was working on finished staining. At least I could be creative when booking the boss's ticket. Of course I'd make sure they got there on time and everything, but multiple connections and huge layovers could be arranged. I'd think of something.

Four o'clock finally rolled around. As I was pushing through the doors of the lab I bumped into Robert.

"Oh, hey Emily. You heading out?" he asked.

"I booked your ticket for the conference in Atlanta next week." I said and then headed straight for the elevators.

"Have a good night, Emily." His hand made a tiny wave for me.

My stomach knotted a little. "Stupid Robert." I muttered.

The day was drier than yesterday but the clouds were waiting. As I hurried towards the forest I suddenly felt very stupid about being so excited. I knew that it had probably just been a hallucination. I knew that. But all the same, I couldn't help it. I really was excited.

The path down to the opening in the forest had dried during the day but the dirt path was still soft and spongy. I nearly took a spill on the steeper part of the trail but some shred of grace kept me upright and mud free.

The hospital stood in the forest opening, exactly as it had the day before. It was clearly no longer used for stashing the people of Huntsville who were plagued by a variety of disorders that left their minds on shaky ground. The door I had burst through the other day swung in the light breeze.

"Hello?" This was meant more for the kids that obviously came here to have sex and smoke pot than it was for some otherworldly being. I didn't get a reply.

The room where the old man had made the wall peel away was at the end of the entrance hall, staring me down. A humorous side of me that I hadn't seen in a few years started playing the theme to *Jaws* in my head. I laughed out loud.

Laughing out loud by yourself makes you feel crazy. Having someone that you didn't expect to actually exist ask you what's so funny makes you think you're even crazier. I stopped dead in my tracks.

The old man suddenly appeared in the doorway. He had the stump of a cigarette in his mouth. Same white t-shirt with the rolled up sleeves. Same Red Sox cap.

He eyed me through the cloud of blue smoke that circled around him. "Surprised you came back."

I nodded. "You and me both gramps."

"Angus. The name's Angus."

"Emily." I stood still and waited for him to do something. I'd never smoked in my life but suddenly wished I did. Having something to do, to make me look like I wasn't waiting on anything, would have been a useful confidence booster at the moment. "So, you live in the wall." Wow. Good stuff, Emily.

He nodded once. "You wanna see it again? Maybe come in and say hello?" He honestly made it sound like he didn't give a shit one way or the other.

"Yeah. Sure." I did not sound nearly as nonchalant as Angus managed.

"Alright then." Same as yesterday, he brushed off the lit end of the butt and lovingly tucked it away in his pack of cigarettes. "Well come on in."

The wall peeled away again, not making a sound as it did. Angus stood beside it like a doorman. "After you."

And then Dumb Emily got behind the wheel. I watched in horror as my feet picked themselves up and stepped through the hole in the wall. Literally, I was walking into a hole in the wall. A cold tingling ran over my skin as if it were looking for the way in. I could feel it sink through my skin and into my muscles before settling like icicles on my bones. It was like I was snowing on the inside. As soon as it had started though, it was over.

I stretched up easily in the white room and moved a little to the side for Angus to crawl in behind me.

The room was a long rectangle with fluorescent lights. The walls were white and the floor was covered in large white tiles. There were no windows or doors. There was one table set up. White, of course. Five white folding chairs circled around the table. Three of them were filled. The contents of each chair were only similar in their shock at my arrival.

"Come on now, have a seat." Angus said as he walked by me. He took the furthest of the two remaining chairs and pointed to the last empty one.

Dumb Emily slammed on the gas and I scooted over to that chair.

"Everyone, this is Emily." Angus introduced me proudly.

"Well, look at you! Aren't you just the prettiest little thing! Angus, where'd you find this cutie pie?" This woman, who sat to my right, had a voice like a baby. Her eyes were bright and dumb like a baby's. But that was where her infantile characteristics ended. The rest of her was squished into a tight sequined bodice and tiny shorts to match. "My name's Dolly." She smiled brightly at me.

I couldn't stop the words. "What the fuck is that you're wearing?"

Her baby eyes suddenly looked wrong. I think she was tearing up a little.

"Oh come on now Dolly! She didn't mean anything by it. Franny said worse to you the first time you met her. You know I think it's just precious." Angus said. He winked at her.

She smiled. The tears dried up before they could even pour. "Oh you."

Angus laughed a little. "Dolly here was a show girl in Las Vegas. Damn good one too. Puts on a little show for us once in a while."

"Oh Angus, stop! You're making me blush!" She giggled in her little baby voice. Okay, maybe one more thing about this moronic earth-bound spook was infantile.

"Yes. Please do stop. First visitor we've ever gotten and you're going to annoy her away." This woman sat to my left. Her hair was a haggard, dried out mess. Her face was pale like she'd never been outside, and the dark rings under her watery blue eyes made it look like she never slept. Her body, no doubt a swell of fatty lumps and extra skin, was covered by a shapeless, baggy dress. I already liked her better than Dolly.

"Hi there, my name's Francine. How'd the hell you find us?" She spit out the question like a piece of hair had gotten tangled around her tongue.

"I really don't have a clue."

She took this answer and chewed on it for a second. "Angus, anyone else ever see you?"

Angus shook his head. "Nah. No one. Not even those kids that get high as kites." He pointed a finger at me. "This one here says it's the year two-thousand and eleven."

The small balding man that sat in the seat between Angus and Francine perked up. "Ah, Miss? Do you happen to know how the VF CORP did in 2009?" His fat little sausage fingers played with one another anxiously.

"No." He looked very disappointed. "Is this actually purgatory? Like you are all dead and unbaptized or some shit?" Who else had ever asked such a question, I wondered.

"Oh heavens no! This may be purgatory and I may have lived in Las Vegas but I attended church every Sunday and I was

13

surely baptized." Dolly's voice was like bubbles. Popping, annoying bubbles.

Francine huffed. "May have been baptized but there was no Sunday service for me. I worked every day I could until the diabetes got too bad. Watch your sugars, it just ain't worth it! The foot pain is unbearable."

"Are you still in pain?" I asked.

She shook her head. "No, not anymore. You don't feel much of anything here. But I tell you, working on that assembly line day in and day out was the fast track to getting old and grouchy."

"What? You didn't just come like that?" Angus quipped.

"Oh shut it, Angus. Life hands you one too many lemons and you just start to get sour."

He nodded. The cool cowboy's way of accepting a momentary truce.

"Fair enough, Franny. I used to drive truck. Those long stretches of road are something else. I couldn't imagine being cooped up in some factory. Would have driven me bat shit crazy." Angus said.

"There you go again, with that back handed compliment. Well I didn't go bat shit crazy, I just got tired. And now I'm stuck with you for pretty much all eternity. The man upstairs just ain't letting up."

Short, balding Doug said nothing.

Angus just looked at me.

"Look, it's been a slice but I think I'll start to shit myself if I stay here much longer." I stood up to leave but something stopped me dead in my tracks. The hole in the wall was gone. "What the fuck? Where'd it go?"

Angus chuckled. Francine sighed. Dolly gasped. Bald man just kept looking disappointed.

"What?"

"I guess you could say that you're just a bit of a surprise to us. And Lord help me if it ain't true, you cuss like a sailor." Angus said.

"Yeah, I'll work on the potty mouth. Now open up that fucking wall, I know you can!" My hands were starting to shake.

Angus laughed again. "Sure. But I meant it when I said you coming here would be a real treat. Please, just sit with us for a bit, let Doug over here ask you a few more stock questions. There ain't no TV here, no newspaper. Hell, it'd be downright depressing if it weren't for Dolly's occasional shows." He shot her another wink. It made her giggle again.

I didn't take my chair. "So, you really think this is purgatory?"

"Yup, we do! I was the first one here. The last year I remember was 1978." Dolly chirped. "Then Angus came to keep me company." She actually batted her eyelashes at him.

He laughed. "Dammit, knew for sure I wasn't getting past St. Peter and those pearly gates. But when I saw her shimmying around this room in that little number I figured maybe the man upstairs had turned a blind eye to me enough times to get me up there. Franny here showing up was what gave it away."

"Yes, and you being here just about convinced me that I'd been sent to hell." Francine shot back.

Angus chuckled again. "I was watching the Red Sox play against the Angels in 1986. Last thing I remember."

"I came in 1991. Had no idea how long we'd been here till Doug came in 2008." Francine added.

"How'd you not kill yourselves?" I paused for a second and then felt really stupid. "Again, I mean."

"Time doesn't move the same way down here. I don't know how to describe it. We know time is passing us by but there's nothing to look forward to and nothing to remember. We don't sleep, there's no meal times. It all just kind of goes." Francine said.

"And I never killed myself." Angus said defensively. "Not saying I lived the best life but I tried to do right by most people and I sure as shit never killed anyone, not even myself. I really don't know why we're here."

"I might have killed myself." Dolly added innocently. "I can't really remember."

"None of us remembers, you twit." Francine snapped. "Hey, where are we right now? What I mean is, we all came from different cities. Which one are we in right now?"

"Huntsville." Blank expressions all around. "It's a small city just outside Vancouver."

"And this is a hospital we're in?" Angus asked.

"Sort of." I laughed to myself. "It's kind of ironic really. I mean, this was where Huntsville threw all of its crazy people. Kind of a purgatory for the living."

"We're in a nut house?" Angus said incredulously.

I nodded. "Creekside. It's been closed down since the sixties."

"Figures." Francine huffed.

I actually felt kind of bad for this pack of misfits. "Angus, I really need to go."

He raised his eyebrows in surprise. "I thought you were just kidding about needing to shit yourself."

"What? Yeah, I was, but I still need to leave! Look, I'll come back tomorrow. Maybe I can sneak some stuff in here." I pleaded.

That was enough. Angus shot out of his seat and went straight for the wall. I don't know how he did it but the wall began to melt away and soon the hole was there again.

"Pack of Marlborough. And some peanuts." For a guy that tried to play it so cool, Angus was suddenly just a little too excited.

I nodded and started to step through the wall but Doug's pathetic yelp made me stop.

"Miss? Could you find out about VF CORP?" He was about two millimetres from begging.

"Yeah, sure. Okay, I really gotta go." I said. I had no idea what the VF CORP was.

I didn't have any friends. I'd made sure of it. Frosty bitch? Maybe. Flake? Never. I do what I say I'm going to do. I would find out about Doug's stock. I would pick Angus up a pack of cigarettes and some peanuts. And I would bring an axe so Francine could at least try killing Dolly.

16

And I don't know why but I was really happy thinking about coming back. Happy and laughing, both in the same day. It'd been awhile.

The Empty Room

The small apartment I shared with Jude was old. The walls and the floors were thick with the mucus yellow that overtook the minds of decorators in the seventies. It had a faded green shag carpet, another gift from that era.

I didn't mind. Everything around me kind of always looked washed out and wasted. I guess at least my home was being honest and upfront about it.

The smell of stale smoke was thick. I knew that even once my aunt died, the smell would never go away. As I threw my keys down on the kitchen counter, I noticed her purse. It was denim and covered in a cheap and tacky assortment of rhinestones. Sitting just inside was a pack of cigarettes.

I grabbed them and twisted them over in my hands. Marlborough.

I could hear the creak of my aunt's recliner as she awoke from her television coma. I heard her shuffle to the kitchen.

"Well, well. Stealing from me? I knew it."

Yeah, you caught me. I paid the rent here, bought the food, and took care of most of the other bills. Her pathetic excuse for a pension covered the television, her bingo habit and the cigarettes I was now holding. Yeah, she was getting the short end of the stick.

"Looks like I just might." I answered as I continued to flip the package over and over in my hands.

She sighed. "Well, it's probably for the best. Help you drop a few pounds."

I felt my mouth almost twitch into a smile as she shuffled back to her chair. Osteoporosis was eating away at her stick thin body and every hinge was nearly crippled with arthritis. I know it made every movement agony for her. But by God, at least she was thin.

"Thanks, Jude." I called after her.

"Don't sweat it, sweetie." she answered back. I had been around her long enough to know that she was actually being nice.

I tucked the cigarettes into my bag and went to my room. Jude's room was at the end of the hall, mine was closer but the empty room was the closest.

I didn't feel like there was much of anything left in me anymore, but what I had seen that afternoon had jolted me somehow. Even so, I still felt like I was on autopilot. Just maybe waking up a bit.

But that room always made me hurt a little. Somewhere deep. Somewhere I couldn't reach to scratch out the pain. Most nights I could walk right by it but not tonight.

I pushed open the door. It squeaked more than the other doors of the apartment. It smelled dusty in here but there was also the faint tinge of vanilla. I sat down on the tiny single bed and grabbed the stuffed bear that slept alone on the pillow.

Normal people would cry if they sat on the bed of their dead baby sister. I wasn't normal anymore though. I didn't cry. I just looked around her empty room and wondered if she was in some white-walled waiting room for all eternity.

Peanuts and Newspapers

The day at the lab was just as boring as any other. A lot of supplies had come in and all day I was fielding questions and complaints from the four graduate students that made up the lab. Where's this stain? I ordered those slides three weeks ago. We're out of paper towel. It was easier than most days to deal with their stupid questions. I had Angus's cigarettes in my bag and I was planning a stop at 7-11 on the way to the old hospital. I felt like Santa Claus preparing for Christmas and I guess this made me more generous than usual with my coworkers.

Even at four o'clock, the day had held on to some warmth. The shock of the icy air conditioning of the overpriced convenience store was very unpleasant. I filled up my arms with magazines, newspapers, candy, chips, drinks and of course, peanuts.

The kid behind the counter was an idiot. There was no denying that. But the fat bitch that stood there waving the miscounted change he had given her was far worse.

"Sorry ma'am. Here, I'll just get you the other five."

"I was already five blocks away when I realized you had shorted me! Do you know how much gas I must have gone through just having to come back for this? I want to speak to your manager!" Her voice was so grating.

"Oh fuck off." I muttered. Guess it was a little louder than I had intended.

"Excuse me?" she said, wheeling around. She looked like a pug dog. Her face was red and squished by the chubby cheeks and double chins.

"I said, oh fuck off."

20

"Who do you think you are? This little shithead was trying to steal from me. That's how they make their money!"

I sighed and shifted my weight to my other foot. Go ahead, Dumb Emily, you've gotten us this far. "Yes, you're right. 7-11's business model is to rip off idiots like you for five bucks a pop. And this genius, this mastermind behind the counter? Well shit, he's actually a billionaire. The only reason he's still working at this crappy job is so that he can dupe assholes like you into driving away without counting your change."

Sweat beaded on her upper lip. It looked like I could have fried an egg on her forehead. She spun away from me, snatched the five dollars out of the cashier's extended hand and wiggled herself out of the store.

I dropped my armful of loot on the counter. The kid just stared at me.

"What?" I snapped.

"I've worked here for two years and tomorrow is my last day. That was the best shit I've ever seen." he said. He really did sound like an idiot. And he stood there with his mouth open.

"Yeah, well, that stupid cunt had it coming." I muttered. Poor kid thought I was sticking up for him. Truth was I just hated people like that woman. Had to shit on someone else to make themselves feel all important.

He laughed. No, he brayed like a donkey. "Yeah, she totally did. Hey, you know what? My boss is an asshole. Take all this shit, on me." He grabbed a bag and started shoving the goods inside. "Yeah, mastermind behind the counter. I'm fucking stoned every day." He handed me the bag with a big, dumb smile. "Grab a Slurpee on your way out, kay?"

"Yeah, thanks."

I actually took him up on the offer. It was cola slush mixed with grape. Julia's favourite. The surgery taste reminded me of her.

I felt stupid. I was waiting in front of a wall in an abandoned institute for the mentally ill.

"Hello?" I called out. Now I felt really dumb. "Fuck this." I muttered to myself.

I dropped the bag of goodies against the wall and rummaged through my bag for the pack of cigarettes Jude had donated to this mission of charitable lunacy.

"Holy smokes, is that all for us?"

I spun around quickly. I hadn't heard him. Angus stared wide eyed at the bag of trash magazines and junk food I had brought for him and the others. And then he zeroed in on the pack of cigarettes in my hand. I thought he was going to cry.

"Are those Marlbourough?" he asked.

"Yeah." I extended my arm and held them out to him. "My aunt smokes them too."

He was about to grab them when something made him think better of it. "Just in case, maybe you should give me those inside."

"Why?"

"I dunno. It just won't work out here. I tried more than once to steal smokes from the kids that come here but it's no good. I just can't seem to grab them." he said.

"Oh. Well, apparently I'm special. Want to try?"

Angus looked like he was steeling himself up for it, like he was really going to give it his all. He licked his lips as he reached out for them. Nothing. His fingers got as much purchase on the pack as fog. He looked defeated.

"Come on, Casper. Open up the wall. Maybe if I'm here to bring all this crap in, it'll work." I said. I was trying to be nice and I think he noticed.

He nodded and then walked over to the wall. The plaster curled away again but this time he stepped through first. I handed him the pack of cigarettes. My arm took on that same tingling, snowing-from-the inside feeling.

"Might as well see if Gabriel or some other archangel comes down to smite me for this before I go in there. You know, give me a running head start."

He nodded in all seriousness. He reached for the cigarettes with the determination of an Olympic athlete. And I almost looked away, it was that intense of a moment. And then my hand was lighter.

His eyes were wide with surprise and joy and his mouth spread into a big, open mouthed smile of pure delight. "Holy fucking mother of Jesus, it works! You can pass us stuff! Thank you Lord for not fucking this one in the ass!"

And I'm the one with the potty mouth.

But I couldn't help smiling. Angus was the picture of elation at that moment. A pony couldn't have made anyone happier.

I grabbed the bag from beside the wall and stepped in after him and handed the goods out. No wonder Santa Claus stuffed himself down the chimneys of desperately poor orphanages. Giving pathetic people what they really, really wanted was kind of awesome. Almost a high.

Everyone noshed away at the junkfood and eagerly flipped through the magazines and newspapers. Even Dolly stuffed her mouth with a few fistfuls of chocolate. They asked me questions about the different things they were reading about but I could only answer so many questions.

"Wonder if you get Wi-Fi down here." I said.

"What's that?" Dolly asked.

"It's used to pick up the Internet." Doug answered without looking up from his paper.

"Oh right! The *Internet!*" Dolly exclaimed. "Doug here told us all about the Internet! Sounds so exciting!"

Francine rolled her eyes at Dolly's enthusiasm. "Sure, we could all get our high school diplomas and then work towards our medical degrees."

Dolly's eyes grew wide. "Really? We could do *that?*"

"Oh hell, of course not!" Francine snapped, but then she stopped. "You can't do that, can you?"

"Probably not legitimately. Even if you could, doubt I'd get any reception down here. Actually, let's see." I fished through my bag for my cell phone. It was an older piece of crap that I rarely used, but the boss of the lab insisted I had one in case he needed something. Most of the time I just left it at home.

"What's that?" Dolly asked, lifting herself out of her chair to have a look.

"It's my cell phone but I can get the Internet on here too if there's any reception." It wasn't that the phone didn't get reception. It just wouldn't turn on. "Sorry, guess I forgot to charge it."

Francine and Dolly settled in their chairs and went back to flipping through magazines. Doug still had his nose in his newspaper and Angus was reading a *Sports Illustrated* magazine.

I wasn't too sure how to approach the subject, but after sitting in Julia's empty room last night, I had to know. "So, I was thinking about how none of you remember how you ended up here. How sure are you that you're dead?"

Angus looked up at me. He knew there was another question coming up shortly. "You just know some things. Trust me, Emily, we're all as dead as they get."

"Did you all just show up?"

"Pretty much." Francine said.

"There were always five chairs so I knew to expect company." Dolly added.

"Huh. I wonder whose chair I'm sitting in." I said quietly.

Angus shrugged. "No rhyme or reason to the times we all showed up. That chair will probably stay empty for awhile."

"Even so…" I stood up. I had lost my nerve to ask for what I really wanted. "I gotta go. But I'll come back tomorrow. Any requests?"

"Scotch and a soda."

We all looked at Doug.

"My stocks are doing well. It used to be my celebratory drink."

That was kinda sad. I just nodded, grabbed my bag and headed for the wall.

The daylight was quickly fading when I left the hospital. It was black by the time I got home.

My aunt snored away in her recliner as usual. Mr. Puggums greeted me at the fridge and whined for his evening meal.

He snorted away as he inhaled his food. It sounded really gross so I left him to it.

I was about to go to my room when I decided to take the first left and visit Julia's room instead.

It needed to be dusted.

I picked up the brown bear I had gotten for her when she was four years old. She took it everywhere with her. She named him Pig. On her first day of kindergarten she had cried for twenty minutes because she wasn't allowed to bring Pig with her.

"Julia! He can't go everywhere with you!" my mom pleaded.

"Why?" she wailed. Julia was five.

"Oh my God, I need to get ready!" My mom tore out of the room in her housecoat and slippers. "You better be ready to go by the time I get dressed, missy!"

Julia sat there and continued to blubber. I had been avoiding the confrontation all morning but it was clear that my mom was at the end of her rope and my sister was still a complete mess.

"Julia. What's the matter?"

"I want to...bring Pig...but mom...won't let me!" she sobbed.

I grabbed her little pink backpack, took out her lunch and stuffed the bear to the bottom of the bag. I replaced her lunch and zipped it all up.

"Now listen, Julia. Pig is scared so he needs to stay in your bag during school."

Her nose was snotty and her cheeks were red as she nodded gravely. I suddenly pictured her whispering to her backpack and decided to nip that one in the bud.

"And he's tired so no talking to him at school. He needs to sleep. You just leave him in there and pay attention to your teacher. Promise?"

"I promise."

"And don't tell mama that he's in there. Just say that you're a big girl and that Pig can stay home. It's a secret that he's in there, okay?"

She nodded even more enthusiastically. I gave her a tissue and told her to clean up her nose goobers. She laughed.

"Well, I guess you're ready to go, missy?" my mom asked from the doorway.

"I'm a big girl and Pig can stay home."

"And I am so proud of my big girl!" she cooed.

Julia waved to me as my mom guided her out through the front door.

"I love you Emily."

I smiled and waved back. "Love you too Julia." I held my finger up to my mouth and made the international symbol for shushing.

She nodded and waved again.

As I held the lonely teddy bear in my lap, I could only think about how much I missed Julia.

Scotch, Soda and Repercussions

I set the bottle of scotch down on the table. The whiteness of the room made the amber liquid sparkle. I looked over at Doug. His eyes were shining.

"Did you bring any soda?" he asked. At that moment I could picture exactly what Doug had looked like at the age of five, asking his mother for a cookie, oh pretty please.

I reached into my bag and brought out the two litre plastic bottle. Doug looked absolutely delighted.

"Two fingers please." he ordered. Normally I rage when anyone asks me to get them anything drinkable or edible because the only person that does it is my boss, and I hate him. Doug, however, had said please and I couldn't help but think that this scotch would be even better to him if poured by someone else and served.

I actually had no idea what two fingers meant so I just poured a sloppy mess of the stuff into one of the short plastic cups I had brought, and then topped it off with soda. Doug didn't even seem to notice the wet sides of the cup. He breathed in the sharp aroma of the scotch that was already hanging in the air and took a refined sip.

I hadn't noticed Angus beside me until he spoke. "That good, huh?"

Doug looked up at us like nothing could ever bother him. "Some people drink to forget. I drink to enjoy."

Angus chuckled beside me. "Em, why don't you have a sit? I'll pour you some."

I took the chair between Dolly and Francine. Angus slid a glass over to me and proceeded to pour glasses for Francine and Dolly, and finally himself. "To whatever the hell is keeping us here, because it also lets this sweet, scotch-bringing little lady come over for a visit once in awhile."

"Here, here!" Doug added in.

I suddenly felt very self-conscious. I took a deep swallow from my glass and it traveled warmly down my throat and sat like a purring kitten in my stomach.

Angus laughed, reached for my glass and poured me another.

"Oh, this is just nasty stuff!" Dolly whined after draining her glass. I guess like me, she too was unskilled in the art of savouring fermented grains. Angus poured her another.

I don't quite know how it happened but before long we were talking about our bosses.

"Mine used to grab my fanny. I'd slap his greedy paws away but he just wouldn't quit!" Dolly said cheerfully. The smile on her face as she described the sexual harassment she had experienced was out of place but I was too drunk to mention it. I looked over at Angus and saw that his face was dark, like he was thinking about punching this probably long-dead boss in the face.

It disappeared as soon as Francine added in her story. "I was on disability from my thirtieth birthday on, so I worked under the table for this *friend* of mine. Turns out the company I was doing some cleaning for was paying three hundred a month to have it done, but I only saw a hundred of it. When I found out later what had been going on, she said that she had to pay for cleaning supplies. Maybe I just knew where to find the deals but some soap and water never ran me two-hundred bucks!"

"So, this friend was kinda like your pimp." Dolly said to no one in particular. We all stopped and looked at her. I thought Francine might slug her for the street-walker reference but she just nodded.

"Yup, that was pretty much it. Except I was getting dirty instead of lucky."

Doug sat forward. "When I was first starting out, I was managing accounts for my boss. He told me that this was only a small lot of his overall clientele and that I was doing it to learn the ropes. Slippery bastard was a fall down drunk but had the good sense to put me in charge of all his accounts. Kept the commissions, the dirty bastard. I know what you mean, getting taken for a ride like that. That's when I went into business for myself."

"Now that's the way to do it!" Angus said a little too loudly. "Bought myself a truck and did as I pleased. Drove the routes I wanted to, charged what I thought it was worth. Never made a better choice."

I smiled and wavered a little in my seat. "I have a degree in microbiology and my boss expects me to get him coffee. That's about the worst of it."

Dolly was the first to say anything. "What's microbiology, hun?"

I must have fallen asleep. I woke up with a fantastic headache and my breath smelled like I'd downed a bottle of hairspray. It hurt to move.

"Morning sunshine!"

I looked up and saw Angus. We were in the old hospital and I was laying on a very gross bed.

"We weren't sure what would happen if you fell asleep in there so while you could still walk we got you out here."

I sat up slowly, bracing my head as I went. "What if someone had come here?"

Angus shook his head. "Maybe a couple kids come in on the weekend but the paper you brought us said it was only Tuesday. No one comes here besides you. And I was out here with you the whole time."

I looked around for my bag and realized that it had been my pillow. I pulled out my cell and saw that it was ten in the morning. I should have been at work by then.

"Fuck."

"Did you oversleep, sunshine?" The smirk was clear in Angus's voice.

"Oh fuck off, this is your fault. You were the one pouring."

Angus laughed. "Pouring into a cup, not your throat."

I really didn't need a lecture on self-responsibility at the moment. I waved Angus off and shuffled out of the hospital. I really could have used a cold, overcast day but instead it was bright and warm. I threw up just outside the old building. I spit a few times, steadied myself and then started towards the trees.

It took me nearly an hour and a half to get to work.

Lynn, the newest and bubbliest addition to the lab, bounced up to me excitedly. I shook my head and held up my hand to push her out of my personal space. "Later." I mumbled.

The neon lights were nauseating and the air conditioning was just too cold. I stumbled to the bathroom and vomited again. This one felt productive. My head started to clear a little more. I rinsed my mouth out and washed my face. It was all helping.

I slogged my way out of the lab and downstairs to the café. I ordered some tea and a cheese scone and sat by the window. I drank the tea and ate the scone precariously. My stomach was not over this yet.

"Emily?"

I looked up. It was Lynn.

"Are you okay?"

I sighed. "I feel like shit. My head is spinning, my stomach is ready to heave even though it's already empty, and I would like to sit here by *myself.*"

She only half took the hint. "Oh, you probably have that nasty bug that has been going around. Hold on, I'm gonna get you some stuff."

I don't where she went but in ten minutes she was back with a big bottle of water, some Gravol and two mystery pills. "Those are ibuprofen, had some in my bag. I got you the rest of this at the drug store."

Lynn annoyed the shit out of me but this was really nice of her. I reached into my purse and pulled out a crumpled ten. "Thanks, Lynn. Here."

"No, no. It's okay."

I looked at her and she stepped back a little. "I know what our prick of a boss pays you. Take it, please."

She smiled and took the bill. "It's not so bad. My parents help out when they can and I babysit one day a week."

I couldn't help but pity her for having to make ends meet with a job meant for fourteen year olds.

"All the same. Look, I just need to sit for a minute and finish my tea. I'll be up soon. Can whatever you need wait about fifteen minutes?"

"Oh, I don't need anything! The boss wanted to talk to you, said he needed a project put together."

I closed my eyes as I answered her. "Okay, sure. I'll talk to him in a bit. Did he say when he needed it by?"

"Uh, I think the conference is tomorrow."

"Tomorrow?"

Lynn nodded.

"Okay, okay. Thanks again." Lynn smiled and headed out of the small coffee shop. I hated our boss so much right then. I fumed as the Gravol and ibuprofen were crushed away by my gut, sending a light buzz to my spinning head. Everything got a little better with each minute I stayed seated in the uncomfortable wooden chair.

I didn't go back up to lab until after lunch. By then my head felt like it was stuffed with cotton balls, but this was an improvement so I couldn't complain. I tried to move quickly from the elevator to the lab but my boss saw me and shouted.

The cotton balls in my brain were suddenly replaced by shards of glass.

"Yeah?"

My boss was a short fuck. He was balding in the strangest pattern. He wore nice clothes that didn't fit him and expensive glasses that didn't suit him. He needed to wear leisure suits. He just looked too out of place in anything else.

"I've got a conference tomorrow. I need you to throw something together for me."

"On what?"

"The stuff Robert has been working on. It's all on here." He handed me a small, silver flash drive. "Just put it into a nice slide show and bring it back to me."

"Why isn't Robert presenting his stuff?"

The boss looked up at me sharply. "He can't make it."

"Whatever. What colour scheme do you want?"

"Well…" he actually pawed at his chin as if that were going to help him think. "The keynote speaker there will be Dr. Kostuk from the Reeds Lab. He gets a lot of funding from the Dalton Foundation and their crest is yellow and blue, so let's go with those colours."

I could tell that he wanted me to ask why he would want that but I already knew. He was hoping to vaguely associate himself with a bigger fish through the subtleties of colour schemes. This was not the first time he had unveiled such genius to me. I just didn't have the patience for it today so I didn't take it any further.

"Fine. How much time do you have to present?"

He reddened at this question. "Well, they're busy and there are a number of speakers…"

"Five minutes?"

He looked down and nodded. The keynote speaker would probably have an hour.

"Alright." I turned and left before he could say anything else.

Thankfully the lab was slow. Only one order came in and everyone except Lynn was listening to a talk on the first floor. I organized five slides with the data the boss had given me. Just as I was about to finish up I heard a group of footsteps and the rush of conversation that accompanies a return from a riveting lecture. Thankfully everyone was well aware that I didn't care and so no one tried to fill me in.

I got up from my desk and started to head out of the bench area when Robert made me stop. He had a confused look on his face.

"What?"

"Uh, hey Emily. Was that my stuff you were just working on?"

I nodded. "The boss wants it in a slide show for tomorrow's conference. Why aren't you presenting it?"

Robert's cheeks flushed. "Uh...uh, it doesn't matter. Thanks."

I should've just left it. Dumb Emily. "Wait a sec. You didn't know he'd be presenting this tomorrow?"

Robert shook his head. "No."

Robert didn't have enough of an ego to say what was really going on but I'd seen the boss do it to him before. He was standing on Robert's work which wasn't horrible in itself. This was the hierarchy on which research was built. But Robert had been here long enough to present his own work and needed to start making a name for himself. Thankfully his work was good enough that it was already speaking for him. All the same, this pissed me off.

I didn't say anything to Robert. I just turned around and went back to my desk. After a few tweaks to the slide show and a little extra work I went back to the boss and handed him the goods.

"Slide show is on the flash drive and here are some cue cards to go with the slides. Good luck tomorrow."

I'd seen the boss work before. I knew he was up to his eyeballs in grant writing and article commentaries. He had no time to actually review what I had written and he was just going to say whatever was already on the cards. This strategy made for choppy speeches where he was figuring out what he was trying to say as the audience was trying to figure out why they were wasting their lunch breaks there.

I didn't feel like a complete bitch. The data was good, and it was being clearly presented. All I did was make sure that credit was given where it was due.

I still had that haze that accompanies a night of drinking. I headed home by five.

The next morning was quiet. I received a few shipments, prepared a staining agent and read an article by Jones. The lab was empty because everyone had gone to the conference the boss was speaking at. I took a long, quiet lunch at a nearby café and read the junk magazines the owner kept around for singles like me. A movie star I had never heard of was pregnant and a director I never cared about was dead.

The isolation of the morning was like a warm blanket. My mind stretched comfortably and safely, thinking about the Jones paper, the pregnant starlet and what I would pick up for the spooky crew today. That all shattered as soon as I stepped in the lab.

They were buzzing like flies on shit.

"Oh my God, can you believe it? I thought our boss was a total douche but that was amazing!"

"And how everyone clapped? You'd think we'd actually produced some worthwhile data here or something!"

I hurried past them and settled at my desk. I was about to turn my computer on when Robert called out to me.

"Emily! Emily!" he was elated. "Thank you so much!"

I looked at him like he was an idiot.

"Uh…the speech! I know you must have written it. No way the boss would have said all that stuff about all of us."

Oh God. I had done it to teach the boss a lesson, and mainly chose to be so horrible because I had been living through a terrible hangover. But this? I hadn't done it for this…gratitude.

"All him. Told me what he wanted and I just made it happen."

Robert looked confused. "But yesterday…you didn't know till you talked to me that he had jacked my stuff."

"Robert, think about it. How could I have written that in without him noticing it? I mean, everyone at least looks at the slides they are presenting before they do. He must have done it."

"But I saw you working on it."

I shook my head. "No. But that's great, glad to hear it went well." I turned my chair around. "I've got a lot of work to do, Robert."

"Oh. Okay. The boss got a great reception. We're heading out for dinner to celebrate. You should come."

As if. "Okay, bye."

I heard him shuffle away as my stomach turned it down a few notches. I felt sick.

I left the lab early again. On my way out, the boss caught me in the lobby.

"Emily. May I speak with you for a moment?"

I looked at him. "What?"

"I wanted to say that your addition to the beginning of the speech, although unexpected, was generally well received." He coughed. "However, I would like to make it perfectly clear that such additions should be run by me. You should not have taken such liberties."

"Well, if you didn't like it why didn't you just decide that when you were going over the notes I had made you?"

He turned red and mumbled something I didn't understand.

"I mean, sure, I didn't need to put it in but I figured you'd run through the speech at least once before going up there. I thought I'd leave it up to you to decide. But I'm glad you decided to keep it in and give Robert and the other students the credit they deserve. I mean, it would have been pretty shitty of you to present someone else's data without acknowledging their hard work. I guess I just figured a guy like you would have wanted that part in." The elevator dinged and the metal doors opened up. "Have a great celebratory dinner!"

Sure, it bothered me that the boss was trying to make sure everyone knew he was top dog and that he called the shots. And true, what he did was something that a lot of lab heads did. I guess I just felt like being awful to him.

I decided on Chinese food for the residents of the defunct Creekside Institute. I even splurged for five fortune cookies.

"Now that was something!" Angus said as he leaned back and patted his gut.

"Oh my, this chow mein is just divine!" Dolly added.

I passed out the fortune cookies. Everyone giggled as they cracked theirs open.

Francine was the first to share. "Ha! You will experience material wealth! Oh sure, sure! These are the robes of a queen!" she said, tugging at her very unattractive and dowdy dress.

"Oh! Expect the unexpected! Now isn't that exciting!" Dolly chirped. I laughed because I knew she was completely serious.

Angus smirked. "Be true to yourself and you will be happy."

"You will find love just around the corner." Doug read.

I looked at mine and for a second my breath caught in my throat.

You will experience great loss but happiness is still possible.

"Hun?" Dolly said. "Are you okay?"

"Uh, yeah. Just says that I'll be happy and prosperous and all that shit."

"Now who comes up with these?" Francine asked. "I mean, what kind of a job is that?"

"I think I would have been pretty good at it." Angus said.

Francine laughed. "Oh yeah? Let's hear it."

He cleared his throat and sat up straighter. "Francine, you will find yourself in a white room with some other dead people. Doug and Dolly, the same goes for you." He turned to me. "Emily? I haven't got a fucking clue."

I couldn't help it. My face cracked a big smile.

"Well done."

He slightly bowed his head. "Why thank you."

A momentary surge of confidence told me it was time to ask something I had been meaning to ever since I'd found this place. "How would you guys feel if I got your last names and where you lived. Stuff like that? So I could find out how you all died."

They all stared.

"Why would you wanna find out a thing like?" Angus asked. His tone was clearly asking *who the hell do you think you are?*

"It's just that none of you remember and none of you seem to know why you're here. I thought maybe if I could look up how you all went, I'd find a pattern or something."

Angus's face didn't change. I was so close to apologizing.

"Yeah, sure. What the hell? Francine May Tate. I lived in Chicago." For some reason, I wasn't surprised that Francine was the first to give me the green light.

"Yeah, I guess you're right, Franny. Can't hurt nothing now." Dolly piped up in her baby voice. "Moira Natalie Seeley."

"Moira?" Angus asked incredulously.

Dolly looked down and blushed. "Yeah, doesn't really suit me, huh? My momma thought the nurse who looked after her when she was having me was the smartest thing ever, so she named me after her."

Angus kept staring. I couldn't help but think about how learning Dolly's real name must have been kind of a like a cold shower. That's correct Angus, this is a person. Not just a play thing, a *Dolly*.

"Oh come on, it's not like Dolly is ever anyone's real name!" I said. He snapped his head back to me and he had on a look that told me to mind myself.

"I was originally from Jersey but I'm pretty sure I was living in Las Vegas when I died." Dolly continued.

"I sure as shit hope so. What other excuse would you have for wearing that?" Francine quipped.

"Douglas Alistair Wells. I ran the Wells Investment firm in Toronto." Little balding Doug didn't even look up from the finance section of his newspaper.

"This ain't right. We don't remember anything for good reason, I'm sure of it." Angus said gravely.

Dolly looked scared. Francine just huffed. Doug kept reading his newspaper.

"Oh come off it, Angus! We're not supposed to be getting these trash magazines and Chinese food hand delivered to us but for some reason it's working. If Emily here wants to learn a little more about why she's the only freak who can see us and this place, well, fine!" Francine shifted her ample self towards me. "I'm not gonna lie, Emily. I'm a little curious myself. Go on and look us up if you want."

Dolly nodded in agreement. "Yeah, I'm wondering about it too."

I looked back at Angus but he wouldn't meet my stare. "Okay, great. So...you all want to know, right?"

Francine and Dolly nodded their heads. Doug kept on reading. And stubborn ass Angus just kept looking down.

"Okay, I gotta go. I'll try to come back tomorrow. Angus?"

He looked up at me like I had just shot his dog. "What?"

I didn't take guilt on too easily anymore. "The wall." I answered impatiently.

He moved silently to the wall, keeping his eyes away from me the whole time. The wall peeled away and just before I stepped through, he caught me by the arm. His grip meant business.

"It ain't right." he said.

I shrugged my arm and his hand dropped away without a fight. "Well, good thing I don't have a clue who the hell you are." I stepped through the hole and didn't look back.

On the walk home I had planned on looking them up right away. But I was tired. Very, very tired. I wrote down their names and the cities they had lived in and fell right into bed.

So gross, I forgot to brush my teeth.

Visit from Julia

I was so tired. The small Asian woman that usually manned the cafe on the main floor of the research facility stared me down as I approached the counter. I had secretly named her Angry Korean Lady because she always looked as though she was about to pull out a shotgun and take someone's head off. Most of the days I succumbed to the need of a latte were without incident but today felt like it had already been decided. I was probably going to get on someone's bad side, might as well be hers.

"What do you want?" she squawked.

"Hot water and lemon." I smiled. It was the cheapest thing on the menu, only twenty-five cents.

"We are out. Pick something else."

"How can you be out? It says right on your board that you sell lemon water. See?" I said, pointing at the menu board behind her.

"We just are. Pick something else." She spoke as if she were spitting on each word before sending them my way.

"Oh, wow. That's too bad. Are you sure? It really does say that you carry lemon water."

"No! No! No!" Each word was accompanied by her tiny, angry fist pounding the plastic counter she ruled.

I sighed. "That's too bad." I left without buying anything.

It really was too bad. I actually kind of wished that I hadn't pestered Angry Korean Lady past the point of no return. I was so tired now without a morning latte.

"Stop being such a baby, just get up!" I grabbed the faded pink quilt off of the tiny bed.

"I don't wanna!" she wailed.

Ah yes, this memory of Julia. This one was especially hard to watch. She was twelve. Maybe if I'd known she'd be gone in just a few short years I would've handled it better.

"Julia! Stop it! You have to go to school!" I yelled at her.

Still laying in her bed, she curled her legs up to her chest and stubbornly anchored her head to her pillow.

"I hate it! I hate the teachers, I hate the students! I hate it!" she sobbed. Julia was always like that. She couldn't help it. Sad, angry, happy, frustrated. For any of them, she cried. It was like her body just couldn't hold in everything she felt.

I was running late already. Julia was starting at a new school. I was twenty-two and starting a new job. Our mom, the glue, had died less than a year ago.

I knew my baby sister was still hurting. She was a mess.

"Julia, please. Get up." I tried gently pleading.

"No."

I should have talked to her. I should have been kind. Instead I lost it.

"That's it!" I shouted. I stalked off to the bathroom and filled up a glass of ice cold water. I stomped all the way back to her tiny room and chucked it at her.

She jolted right up from the water and screamed.

"Now get up! I'm so sick of this Julia!" I yelled.

Jude was in her room but there was nothing that could wake her from her *Rivotril* coma.

And then that face. Julia had always been a sweet child. She loved everybody and everybody loved her. She was never mean, but at that moment, Julia hated me.

"Get out of my room." she said. Each word sounded like it had just jumped out of a cold hell.

"Are you going to get ready? I have to go!"

"Leave me alone."

"Oh come on, Julia! Get this straight. You have to go to school!" I knew I should have backed down. She was hurting and I had just dug my fingers into that hurt, but for some reason, I wouldn't stop.

She jumped out of bed and rushed at me. She slammed all of her weight against me and pushed me to the wall. She held her forearm across my throat and pinned me there. At that moment, sweet Julia was nowhere to be found. "You're not my mother, now get the fuck out of my room."

I felt like someone had just hit me in the gut. That might have hurt less.

She backed off of me. She was only twelve but she was tall enough to get in my face and strong enough to hurt me. In more ways than one.

She went to her bed and sat down on the wet mattress with her back to me. Her shoulders slumped.

"You're right." I said quietly. "I'm not your mother. She's dead."

And I left her. Alone. And in wet pyjamas. She didn't go to school for the rest of the week.

"Emily?"

My head bounced up from my desk. I had fallen asleep. I looked up and saw Robert looking down at me. His face looked weird.

"What?"

"Uh, sorry. You fell asleep."

"Wow, thanks Robert. You really did me a solid. How about next time though, you just mind your own business?" I started shuffling my papers and went back to looking at my computer screen. I had no idea what I was reading.

"Sorry, I was just leaving. I didn't want to leave you here over night." he said quietly.

I looked at the tiny clock in the bottom right hand corner of my computer screen. It was already eight-thirty.

"Oh." I said a little quieter this time. I looked up at Robert and realized that this little punk had actually managed to make me feel bad. "Sorry. Thanks."

I think he smiled at me. What an idiot. I treat the dog shit on my boots better than I treated him because once I was finished stepping in it and then scrapping it off, me and the shit parted ways. Robert had to see me every day and he took it.

"Yeah, it's okay." he said. "I'm getting some dinner before I go home. Do you want to come with me and grab something? I could drop you off after?"

It was too late to go to Creekside. Angus would understand. Franny would be choked but she'd get over it. A morning latte could keep me going all day but I had to go fuck it up this morning and now I was hungry. No, it was past that, I was starving. My stomach growled at the thought of food. Stupid organ.

"Sure." I turned my computer off and left the pile of papers scattered on my desk. It was weird for me to leave such a mess but I didn't care. Not today. Not after that bitter visit from Julia.

"What do you feel like?" Robert asked.

"I don't care." Such a lie. And then I realized that *I don't care* could be misconstrued as *I don't care, I'm just happy to be with you.*

"Okay, how about sushi?"

I wanted to scream at him about how much I hated sushi. But that was a lie. I wanted to tell him to piss off, leave me alone, I have things to do. Another lie.

"Okay." This was self-preservation speaking now. Say as little as possible. Order your stupid sushi and go home.

The restaurant was warm compared to the cold wind that had whipped by us on the short three minute walk there. And there she was. Angry Korean Lady, overseer of the ordering counter.

She hadn't forgotten me either.

"What do you want?" she glared at me.

Robert didn't seem to notice. "Heya Nancy! How's it been here tonight?"

I couldn't believe it. Angry Korean Lady smiled at him. "Welcome, Robert." Sounded more like she said *Obert*. "Would you like the special today?" She held an arm up to showcase the dark chalkboard menu beside her.

He read it over carefully. "Oh wow, this looks delicious Nancy! Yes, I'd love one of those, thank you. And whatever Emily's getting."

"No, Robert. That's okay. I'll get my own."

He looked hurt. I glanced at Nancy. Self preservation took over again. She looked liked she was seriously considering chopping my head off.

"I mean, only if you let me buy you your coffee tomorrow."

He beamed. How desperate could he be? Sure, he dressed like a homeless man, always shuffling around in clothes too big for him. But other than that, I had no idea why he was single. It wasn't that guys weren't on my radar. It was just that my radar was turned off. But I had eyes. Robert was kind of good looking. And really smart. He would be running his own lab soon, not even a question. And despite my best efforts at embodying the very concept of bitch, he was still nice to me.

"Emily?"

I shook myself back into the moment. "What?"

"Did you want to eat here or get it to go?" he asked.

"Oh. Um, how late is this place open?"

"Ten." Nancy's answers were so short and quick, it was like she was hacking them out instead of speaking them.

I looked at her. She clearly still hated me. "Okay, well, here. Unless you have to go." I looked back at Robert.

He was smiling. "No, no. Here is really good. And Nancy here is a wiz. She's actually faster at making sushi than she is at making coffee. We'll have lots of time to eat it before she needs to close up."

I looked back at Nancy, suddenly wanting her okay. She was looking appreciatively at Robert. Not like she wanted to write his name all over her diary. It was more maternal. Like she was proud of him.

He paid and we took a small table by the window.

"You must have been pretty tired today. You were out for like three hours." he said.

I glared at him. "Haven't been getting enough caffeine I guess."

"Oh I know! The entire lab is completely addicted to coffee! I swear Nancy puts some coke in it or something." He laughed at his own joke.

"Yeah, right. So Angry Korean Lady works both jobs? Wow."

He looked confused for a second. He even twisted his head to the side. It made him look like a thoughtful parrot. "You mean Nancy?"

I nodded.

"Oh no, she owns both places. She runs the coffee shop in the day. Her husband works here during the day. He goes home and looks after their kids while she finishes up here."

That insight into Angry Korean Lady's life suddenly made me feel like shit.

"Crazy." I mumbled.

"Yeah, I know, right? I feel so lazy compared to her."

I felt my eyes open a little wider. "You? You're like the hardest working person in that lab. Seriously, I don't know why you're still there. You could have your own lab if you wanted. I'm surprised you haven't been offered one already."

He smiled shyly and looked down at his hands. Nancy dropped off two cups of tea before zipping back to the kitchen. He grabbed his cup and drank nervously.

"What?"

He looked up at me. "What, what?"

"When I asked about the lab, you got all shady. Are you going somewhere?"

A nervous smile twitched across his face. "Yeah, I got an offer. Pretty good too. I'm just...thinking."

I dropped it. I never wanted to talk about anything with anybody and despite being so self-involved, I could tell when someone else was feeling the same way.

"What about you? I know you were working in Boyd's lab in Vancouver before he retired. The way he went on about you I was sure you'd end up in grad school."

I could actually feel the ice creeping back over me. I hadn't even noticed I'd thawed.

"Yeah, guess I'll just stay a lowly lab assistant."

"Oh no, I didn't mean it like that. I just..."

I was already up and out of my chair. These weren't conscious actions. Self-preservation pushed me out the door towards home. I pulled my sweater around me as soon as I got outside, realizing I'd left my jacket on the back of the chair. Fuck, fuck, fuck.

No, I wouldn't go back to get it. I broke into a jog and by the time I turned onto my street, I was running.

After bursting into my apartment, I felt the sting of tears in my eyes. I was coming apart at the seams and no one could see that. I was angry enough that I had to be present for it.

I stumbled into Julia's room and slammed the door behind me. I curled up with the friendless teddy bear on her bed and started sobbing. I could have solved a tiny African village's water crises that night. I don't remember falling asleep.

Even though I was in her room, crying on her bed, Julia let me be that night.

Bring the Baby Here

I was beat the next morning. No dreams, but I still felt like I had been going all night. I felt like I had been drinking. When I remembered what had set me off, I felt the day-after shame of it all.

I hoped Robert turned out to be a total dick. I hoped he'd grabbed my jacket and gave it to some homeless person or threw it in the trash. Anything but give it back to me.

I was not that lucky. On my desk was my jacket, neatly folded. There was a note on it. He had the printing of a five year old. The letters were big and clumsy.

Hey Emily,

I'm really sorry. I didn't mean it at all the way it sounded. You're the smartest person in this lab and everyone knows it. See you next week.

Robert

Next week?

I turned around and saw George walking into the lab. He met my eyes for a second before looking up. Down. To the right. Anywhere but back at me. George was the oldest grad student in the lab and the dumbest. He was so irritating because he was one of those grad students that had pursued further education because he wasn't good for anything else.

"George." I barked.

He stiffened. "Oh, hey Em! How's it going?"

"Emily."

"What?"

"Fuck, never mind! Where's Robert?"

He looked confused for second, like who's Robert? His eyes lit up when he finally matched the name to a face in his big, dumb head. "Oh, Robert! Him and the boss went to a conference in Atlanta. Didn't you book the tickets?"

Suddenly I remembered. I had booked Robert a first class seat and the boss got one in coach by the bathroom. *Irritable bowel syndrome,* I'd said to the travel agent. It was all lab money anyway, but now I was seriously regretting my little dig. Robert would think I had tried to do him some sort of a favour.

Oh well. Whatever. It's not like Robert didn't deserve it. This lab was getting the best grants because of him. I probably owed this crappy job to him too.

I went back to my desk and sat down. It was such a mess. I started shuffling the papers around and piling them up. I couldn't focus on any of it.

And then a baby wailed.

I spun around in my chair as if a shotgun had just gone off. Everyone was circled around someone and thankfully no one saw me. I must have looked guilty of something.

I moved a little closer, trying to see through the wall of bodies. It was Jenny.

Jenny had been a grad student here last year. She'd gotten married and knocked up. Pissed the boss right off. For that reason alone, I would have liked her but there was something else. She reminded me of Julia.

She was much smaller than Julia had ever been, much more delicate looking. But she had blond hair like sunshine. And pretty, big blue eyes. And she was nice. Even to me.

I stood up and took a few cautious steps towards the group. Jenny still hadn't seen me yet. Her smile was electric; her face was like a basket of roses. She looked so happy.

"Emily!" she squealed. "Come, meet Marley!"

My hands twitched at the memory of the first and only baby I had ever held. I tried to force myself to smile but my face just twisted uncomfortably. I must have looked like I was getting ready to eat the baby.

"Hi Jenny. You look great." I said. I could feel George gawking at me. I shot him a quick look and he stopped immediately. I knew that me being civil with anyone, let alone complimentary, must have been a shock for George.

If Jenny noticed, she hid it completely. "Oh, it's so good to see you Emily!" She gave me an awkward but no less friendly one-armed hug. The little baby in her arms made some odd gurgling noise like a plugged drain.

"I didn't forget you!" she cooed at the baby. "Marley, this is Emily!"

She tilted the baby a little so I could see better.

I knew I had gasped.

"Emily? Are you okay?" Jenny asked. She looked worried.

I smiled and nodded. The tears were coming up now. I only had a few seconds to clear out. "Yeah, she's just so pretty."

"He." Jenny gently corrected me.

A choked laugh escaped me. "Still pretty."

She beamed. "I know, right? Do you want to hold him?"

I took an involuntary step back and held my hands up. "I...feel like I might be coming down with something. Think I'm gonna go home actually. Next time for sure."

Jenny nodded sweetly. "Okay! Feel better Emily."

I grabbed my bag and my jacket and got out of there.

It was a really nice day. I thought about heading back to Creekside and then decided against it. I still hadn't looked up the information on anyone. Francine and Dolly would have fallen for my lies of it taking longer than I had first thought but Doug wasn't *that* dead. He'd probably heard of Google.

I went to the park and settled down on the grass. The sun was so warm on my face. I squeezed my eyes into slits as I looked up at the unusually bright blue sky hanging over Huntsville. On most days this place was soaked by nine in the morning.

The first day I'd met Julia was just like this. And just like her. Perfect.

"When are they gonna be here? You said they'd be home today!" I shouted.

"Can it!" Jude barked back. "They'll get here when they get here. Grab my purse, would ya?"

I don't quite know why, but I always did what grownups told me to do when I was young. I hated them but for some reason I still believed that I had to do what they told me. I stomped into the kitchen, like only a petulant nine year old can, and stomped back. I held out Jude's purse but she didn't take it.

"Grab my smokes and my lighter out of there, would ya?" Her eyes were glued to the screen. Jeopardy.

If it had been in my vocabulary yet, I would have let a big *fuck* tear out of my throat just then.

I had found the lighter when I heard the key twist in the front door's lock. I dropped my aunt's bag and ran to the door. I yanked it open before my mom even had a chance to take her key back.

"Mom!" I yelped.

She wrapped one arm around me as I threw my arms around her waist. "Oh, Emily!" I felt her dip and kiss my head. "I missed you!"

"I missed you too!"

"Honey, do you want to meet your little baby sister?"

I looked up at her like she had just offered me iced cream and a pony. "Yes!"

She smiled. She was so beautiful, especially when she smiled. "Okay, go on now, sit down on the couch and you can hold her."

I tore off and dived into the old green couch. I twisted myself till I was sitting upright and started patting my thighs excitedly. "Bring the baby here!" I hollered.

My mom smiled as she sat down beside me. "Okay, now Emily, she's still little so you have to be gentle with her."

I nodded gravely. This was serious now.

My mom put the swaddled baby in my arms and adjusted me until my baby sister was safe.

"She's so pretty." I marvelled. Even at nine, I knew this baby was beautiful.

My mom laughed a little. "Yeah, she sure is. Haven't seen a baby this beautiful since I brought you home."

That made me smile. Later on I would compare pictures of the two of us as babies. I was definitely not as pretty, but that never diminished how happy I felt when I thought of my mom telling me this outright lie. Only a mother.

"Now, you're so smart and such a wonderful daughter, I know you are going to be the best big sister ever," my mom said encouragingly.

I nodded without taking my eyes away from this perfect baby's face. "What'd you name her?"

"Julia."

I nodded again. "Yeah, she looks like Julia."

My mom laughed. I didn't realize what was funny but I loved the sound of my mom's laughter so much that I didn't care. "You'll help me take care of her, right?"

"Oh yes." I said.

I wonder if my mom would have considered this promise I made to her at the age of nine horribly unfulfilled by what would happen to this perfect being only fifteen short years later.

A violent shiver rocked down my spine. It was cold.

"Fuck." I muttered. I had fallen asleep in the park. It was still light out but the day was rapidly rushing into the evening. I had slept there all day.

I walked home slowly as I mulled over just how much Marley had reminded me of the first day I had met Julia. Both such pretty babies.

No Patterns

It was Saturday. Normally I'd head to the lab to check on mice or some cells but there wasn't any of that happening. I had the day off. Then I saw the list of names and cities on my bedside table. Being idle never worked well for me. Especially in the last few years. I got straight to work.

It didn't take long to find Francine and Doug's obituaries. Annoyingly, they were the polite kind that didn't mention how the person had ended it all. But each hinted at *suddenly*.

I read through Francine's obituary again. *Survived by brother James.* I looked up his contact information and called his home in Chicago. This month's long distance bill was going to be hell.

A gruff voice answered on the fourth ring in a rough *hello*.

"Hi, my name's Emily. My mom is Doreen Simmons. She's getting on and asked me to look up some of her friends that she wanted to get in touch with. One of them is Francine May Tate but I can't seem to find her in the phone book. Would you happen to be of any relation?" Not bad, I thought to myself.

The line was quiet for a minute. "Doreen, you said?"

"Yes." I suddenly hoped that Francine hadn't actually known any Doreens. I didn't.

"Well, I'm sorry to pass this on, but Franny's not with us anymore. She passed away twenty years ago." His voice was genuinely apologetic.

Now I felt like crap but I was in too deep. "Oh my gosh, I'm so sorry! My mom had said they'd grown apart."

"Well, as much as I loved her, Franny tended to make that happen without much work."

"Look, I know this is none of my business but would you tell me how she died?"

The line was quiet again. A heavy sigh told me he was still there and seriously considering telling me. "She gave herself too much insulin. Easy to do I guess but she was alone so much that we didn't find her until it was too late."

"I'm so sorry. My deepest sympathies." How many times did I hear those exact words twice upon a time?

"Thank you. And mine to your mother." he answered kindly.

"I will pass those on, thanks." I felt like crap but what was I supposed to have said? *Hey, you'll never guess where I bumped into your dead sister! Huntsville of all places!*

I stopped for a moment before continuing on. Francine was actually dead and although I had expected as much, I now had a person to go with the name and the method of death. I could feel a deep pain flare up within me as my body and mind remembered this feeling. I took a slow breath and exhaled completely as if that could extinguish something within.

Doug was next. He was actually much easier. Because he had died so recently, I managed to find an article on his passing. *The Passing of a Legend,* it was called. I would have bet money that I had an article on the wrong guy except for the picture. As much as he had paid the photographer to make him look impressive, it was still Doug. He might as well of saved a couple of bucks and had this shot done at Sears for all the good it did him. There was no one talented enough to make this small, balding man look fierce.

The article was short and had what I'd needed. Doug had died of a heart attack. The article also said that the paramedics had found him in the bathroom. I knew that meant on the can, otherwise they would have said shower, but I had already decided that I would leave that bit out. He had no surviving family. I found myself hoping that with all the money, Doug had been able to at least buy the occasional date.

I'd left Dolly last. There was no obituary. I wasn't surprised. Dolly had died so long ago that I was pretty sure no mention of her could be found on the Internet. I'd hoped that she had been some crazy awesome Las Vegas stripper whose death was a big deal, but there was nothing.

I really didn't want to go back to Creekside before I had something for each of the willing participants but I also didn't want to stay away. I knew that any normal person would have stayed away from that place but I guess I wasn't normal anymore. I don't know what it was about them but I felt better when I was there.

I walked past my lab, paused for a second and thought about going in but decided to just keep on going. I came up to the 7-11 and thought long and hard about a peace offering for Angus. I didn't do anything wrong. They all could have told me to go to hell but they didn't. They wanted to know what had happened to them just as much as I needed to know. But Angus would still be upset with me and I wanted to make it right somehow.

I considered a Penthouse or Playboy but then thought it through a little more. Even if the guy could get it up in purgatory, it was one room that he shared with three other people. There wasn't even a bathroom he could excuse himself to. And if he couldn't, well...why remind him of that fact? Angus had a swagger about him like a cowboy. He didn't need to be reminded that his stud days were well behind him.

I settled on another pack of Marlborough, some more peanuts, chips, pop, licorice and a few newspapers. As I dumped my armful of snacks on the counter, I caught sight of a setup of novelty lighters. They weren't as great as the kinds with magically undressing women but I still found them funny in a campy sort of way. They were little revolvers. Yeah, the cowboy would like one.

I smiled to myself as I pushed open the doors and headed out to the old hospital.

"Hey!"

I turned around. The gangly kid that had been behind the counter the other day was walking towards the 7-11 in his regular clothes. Hoody, tight skinny jeans and a skateboard. I have to admit, I didn't think he'd have the coordination for that sport.

He was all smiles. "Whoa, you must be such a stoner, you're already resupplying." He hee-hawed as he looked at the fat bag I was carrying.

"No, I wish."

He eyed me carefully for a second. "Really?"

"Sure. Are you still working here?" I didn't know why he suddenly looked so interested and a change of topic seemed in order.

"Nah, just coming by to pick up my last check before the boss does inventory and tries to stiff me. But seriously, I've got some dope. That's my new gig. Good stuff too. I'd sell it to you at cost. Give you the fat-bitch-ass-kicker discount!"

Ladies and gentlemen, may I present Dumb Emily. "Sure. I've got ten bucks, how much will that get me?"

"Tell you what. I've already got two fatties rolled. They're yours." He reached into the pocket of his hood and pulled out a small plastic baggie.

I handed him a crushed up ten from my pocket and took the plastic baggie. I'd never tried this shit in my life. Whenever it came up in school, I'd been too busy. My excuse now was that nobody offered anymore. Guess Dumb Emily just didn't want to miss out on all these experiences just because the rest of me was a pill.

"Thanks. Be careful, eh? Watch out for feds or something."

Hee-haw! "Feds? Do we even have those in Canada? Nah, maybe some asshole on a horse but I'm not too worried. They'll just steal whatever stash I've got on me and let me go about my business. They're as high as the rest of us."

This kid was getting better every second. "Alright. See ya."

"Yeah, see you around."

As I walked to Creekside, I wasn't too sure what I was planning to do with my purchase. I shoved it in my pocket and forgot about it.

The building looked a little brighter today. I knew it was just the sun being out for a blessed and rare occasion but it was still nice. The crude graffiti down the entrance hall didn't seem so bad. The lingering smell of piss wasn't as strong.

"Finally decided to grace us with your presence, I see." Angus leaned against the doorway of the room at the end of the hall.

"Hope time doesn't move like that for you usually. I've only been gone two days." I shot back.

"Even still, getting everyone's panties bunched up like that and then leaving them hanging. Not very nice." Angus was really good at looking like he didn't give a rat's ass.

"I brought you a present."

He casually lifted his eyebrows in mock surprise. "Is that so?"

I was about to fish out the lighter when I remembered what had happened the other day with Jude's smokes. "Maybe I could go in and see everyone first? You can't grab anything out here anyways."

He sucked away on a long, white cigarette, continuing to look as if he had all the time in the world. I guess he did.

Finally he rubbed off the cigarette's burning end and tucked away the precious stem.

"Still being frugal with those?"

"Habit." he answered as he tucked the pack back into his sleeve, as usual. "Alright, let's go."

The wall opening up was starting to look normal. That couldn't be a good thing.

"Angus? Are you the only one who can do this?"

He shook his head. "Nah, they can all do it. Just no reason to come out. Can't go too far anyways and it's nicer in there."

I went in first. Francine, Doug and Dolly all shot their heads up once they realized that Angus wasn't alone.

"Emily!" Francine exclaimed. She actually seemed happy to see me. I winced when I remembered what I had promised to find out about her. "Come on, have a sit!"

I forced a smile and went to table where I spilled out the contents of the plastic bag. I moved a few things around until I found what I was looking for.

Dolly gasped. "Emily, hun. Why'd you bring that?"

"It's a present. For Angus." I turned around, still holding the lighter in my hand.

He smiled. "Well I'll be damned." He took the lighter from my hand carefully. Guess he didn't wholly trust this loophole I'd made possible. Once it was in his hand and he could feel the weight of it, his smile widened. He clicked the lighter and I heard Dolly gasp as the tiny revolver shot out a lick of fire.

"It's just a lighter?" she asked. It could have been a five year old asking.

"Yeah, not to worry Dolly. It's just a lighter." He looked back at me. The smile had reached his eyes. "Well, I have to say, this was real sweet of you."

I nodded. "You're the first person I thought of when I saw it."

Apology gifts work...even with the dead. We both took our seats and everyone happily munched away at the junk food I'd brought. I could tell that Francine was eyeing me from time to time, just waiting for the perfect moment to ask. I should have saved her the anxiety but now that I was there, I really did see what was wrong about it. They probably didn't remember shit about dying for a good reason, just like Angus had said.

"I know it's only been a little while but you didn't happen to get anywhere with, well, you know, what you wanted our names for?" Francine was being coy. It seemed very strange coming from her.

I could have said no. I could have lied and told her that moths had gotten to every scrap of history about her and that there was no way to find out a thing. I could have put it off like calling someone back, over and over. Eventually, most people would take the hint. But I couldn't. Not really. This was never mine to hold back.

"Yeah, I did."

Francine scooted to the edge of her chair. "Well? What'd you find out?"

"You want me to say it in front of everyone?" I don't really know why I asked that.

"That bad, huh?"

"What? No! Not at all, I just...if you guys don't care, I'll tell you all where I'm at right now."

"Well I don't care, go ahead! Not like I'm taking a shit in front of anyone." Francine's eyes were bugging out a little bit now. It made her even less pretty.

"I don't mind, either." Dolly chimed in.

I looked at Doug. He wasn't even listening. "Doug? So?"

He flipped down the big newspaper he had his nose stuffed into. "What? Oh, yes, go on."

I was off the hook from everyone except probably Angus. I couldn't handle looking at him right now so I just pretended like he wasn't glaring ominously at me.

"Okay, well, first off, Dolly. You passed away the earliest so I haven't been able to get a handle on your records yet."

Her shoulders slumped a little. "It's okay, I know you tried."

"Hey! Dolly, she just said *yet*. She'll keep looking, not to worry." Angus patted her shoulder a little and then looked back at me. I couldn't tell if he was glaring at me or pleading.

"Yeah, that's right. I'll keep checking." The eyes got a little softer, a little easier to look away from. "Now, Doug. Turns out you died of a heart attack."

He looked at me like I had just told him ducks like water. He nodded and then went back to reading his paper.

Now that was the letdown I needed. He didn't care. Suddenly I felt better about everything.

"Okay, and Francine. Took some hunting but apparently you took too much insulin."

Francine's face was suddenly a big mix confusion, anger, sadness and disappointment. Now I realized how I should have gone about lying. I should have made up some crazy death like she was shot while in the arms of her boss or that she caught some rare tropical disease while hiking to Machu Picchu.

Anything but this. This death was so little, so easily accepted and forgotten by most. No articles would have been written about it. No intense investigation to follow. The day started out like any other. There was nothing foreboding about it.

"Why didn't they just give me some sugar?"

She wasn't looking at me. It was hard to tell if she was asking me but I decided to answer anyways. This was the part I really didn't want to bring up. "Well, you were alone when it happened. You fell into a coma and when they found you it was too late."

Her lips were twisting and puckering like they were trying to keep something nasty from coming up again.

It was Angus that finally broke the silence. "Hell of a peaceful way to go, Franny. Anyone should be so lucky as to just head off to sleep."

Sounded like a stupid thing to me but the effect it had on Francine was like magic. The wandering look in her eyes was gone in a second, like he'd brought her back from some desolate corner of her mind. Whatever else Angus may have been, at that moment it was clear to me that he was also a good man.

Father

I felt exhausted when I got home. But good. It was easy around them.

I would have gone straight to bed but Jude called out to me from her recliner.

"There's a card for you on the table." she said. Her fingers were like the knotted branches of an old tree, abused by too many winters. They bumped up and down on Mr. Puggums' bony body.

"Okay. Thanks."

"Hey, hun? Happy Birthday." She didn't look away from the TV as she said it but that didn't bother me. It was actually her detachment that I took solace in. Neither of us had to feel bad about ignoring the other.

The kitchen was clean as usual. Jude barely ate and when I did, it wasn't much. A pack of cheap noodles, a banana or some cereal. Such appetites didn't really result in too many dishes.

The card's envelope was pink this year. I got one every year on my birthday. I had never met my dad but he never forgot my birthday. Not really sure why he bothered. We didn't meet for lunch, he didn't tease me about boys, I never visited. I didn't even have a picture of him. I know he had some of me but nothing recent. I probably looked the same.

My mom had always been careful to give me my birthday card when Julia wasn't around. It wasn't that Julia was a selfish child but she would have cried about it. Not knowing her father hit her hard. I wanted to just give her my cards, I didn't care about them. Once the five bucks they always contained was tucked away in some cheap plastic wallet or underneath my mattress, the card was garbage.

One time, when I was fifteen, the card was knocked from its customary place of display on my window sill to the floor. I didn't notice. It got crushed and torn and I should've thrown it away but I just didn't care. I was busy studying or playing with Julia. My mom found it. She'd never made me feel bad before that day, not once. All she had to do was rescue it from my floor like it was a wounded bird. She sniffed a little as she carried it away to the kitchen where she carefully taped it back together.

"I know it doesn't mean much now, Emily. But family is all you have sometimes." She was crying. I had made her cry.

"It's just a card." I said. I didn't want to take on those tears. I wanted some other reason for their arrival besides my own indifference to a father I didn't know.

"Do you see anyone else in this house getting cards? These tell you that someone out there is thinking about you. That someone gives enough of a shit to remember your birthday." Her voice was so quiet. Barely above a whisper.

"He doesn't visit, he doesn't call! Really gives a shit? Why doesn't he come here if I'm so important? It's because I'm not!" The louder I yelled, the more I knew I was wrong. But maybe I could drown out her accusatory whimpers.

She did stop crying but she wouldn't look at me. "You're right."

I didn't know what to say, so I just left. The mended card was waiting for me on my bed when I got home.

Memories of my mom were now barely breathing but this one had survived.

This year's card had a little girl sitting in front of a cake with smiling cats and dogs. Figures. He maybe saw me once when I was a baby and even he knows I don't have any friends within my own species.

Happy Birthday to a Special Girl. The neat print of the card company looked cold and insincere compared to the scrawling in dark blue ink. *Love dad.*

And five bucks. For so many years these cards were minor hiccups in my life, unfortunate but mostly harmless reminders of the disjointed family I was a part of. I loved my mom and Julia, and they loved me, so I guess it used to be easy to dismiss these annual cards. But I was alone now and the cards had gotten harder and harder to ignore.

"Hun? You okay" Jude cawed from her recliner.

Fuck. I was crying. "Yeah, I'm going out for a bit."

"Where to?"

"Just a walk."

"Okay. Hey, will you pick me up some smokes? That pack you stole really threw off my budget and I'm almost out."

"Yeah, I'll be back in a bit."

The night air was cold and felt so good, like a shock to bring the focus of my thoughts back. I was coming apart, there was no denying that now. I had just cried over a birthday card.

Mr. Greene and Julia

I tried to forget the time I saw Julia with him. I had come to Julia's school to drop off a paper she'd forgotten and the school secretary told me that Julia had just finished gym. The gym was empty except for Mr. Greene and Julia, off in a corner. His hands were all over her as they kissed. I felt like I was going to be sick. I bent over and took a few deep breaths to keep from passing out. When I looked up again, Julia was gone and Mr. Greene was heading back to his office. My rage clouded my thoughts. If I'd been smart, I would have called the cops right then. Instead, I went to the gym teacher's office.

"Mr. Greene?"

He turned around and smiled when he saw me. Looked like any other high school gym teacher. Kind of athletic but gaining enough middle age chub over it all to make him only a poor reflection of what he once was. And my sister, my beautiful and popular sister, had fallen for it.

"You're Ms. Cameron, right? Julia's sister. Yes, I remember you from parent-teacher interview night." He raced towards me with his hand out.

I took a step back and threw my arms out in front of me. "Keep your fucking hands away from me and from Julia."

He straightened at that. His mouth opened and closed a few times but if he had said something, I didn't hear it.

"You piece of shit! She's fifteen! What the fuck is the matter with you?"

"Emily?" I whirled at the sound of her voice. I hadn't even heard the door open.

Julia stood there. Her hair was wet, probably just came from the showers. No makeup, in a baggy sweatshirt and pants. She was still beautiful. Her big blue eyes were pleading with me.

"Julia, get out of here. I'll come get you in a second."

"Emily, wait." She came in and closed the office door behind her. "He didn't do anything."

And that was too much for me. She was *lying* for this piece of crap. "Julia, I saw you!"

Her cheeks went bright red. I could almost hear the thought of *so much for that approach* whiz through her mind. "What I meant was, I went after him."

"Julia, you're a kid! I don't care if you danced around naked in front of him, it's fucking sick what he's doing!"

"Emily, we're in love."

Now that stopped me for a second. I spun around and looked at him, cowering in the corner. "You told a fifteen year old that you loved her? When were you planning on bringing her home to the wife? Don't you have a kid?"

"Emily! Stop it! We were gonna wait until I was done high school. For me! I don't need the reputation of being a home wrecking slut for my last two years of school!"

I couldn't believe what I was hearing. Julia was not stupid but right then I would have put Mr. Puggums' IQ ahead of hers. "So what, you guys will just keep fucking in his office until then?" I turned back to him. "Are you going to give up sticking it to your wife until then or fuck them both?"

"Emily! Don't do this! Stay out of it!" I could hear from her voice that she was near tears.

I pulled her close and wrapped my arms around her. "You're so much better than this, Julia." I took a step back and held her face in my hands. "He will never, ever deserve you."

A few tears fell down her red cheeks. "Just don't say anything, please? Don't call anyone."

The regret I have for my next words stays with me like a bad ache. Always there. Not strong enough to kill me. Not weak enough to let me live in peace. "Okay. I won't. Not even Jude."

She laughed a little. "Especially not her."

I nodded. "Come on. Let's go."

I should've admitted it to myself that this wasn't over when she twisted her head around as we left Mr. Greene's office to look at him. But I was pathetic. I was weak. I wanted to believe that this was all a mistake and that she would actually move on now that I knew about it. I told myself that the thrill of sneaking around wasn't there anymore. That she didn't need him anymore.

I may have been wrong about her, but I wasn't about him. He didn't need her anymore. The stakes had gotten too high.

Mouse Ten

It was kill day.

Most of the researchers had a nicer way of saying it like *harvest.* I guess that makes sense. They really were harvesting the tiny bodies of mice for organs, tissues and God knows what else. But to me, who had no personal investment in the research, it was kill day.

It was okay though. These particular mice had been on an experimental chemotherapy and they were sick. It would be a relief to let them go peacefully.

This was George's project. Most of the time I just did the leg work of the research on my own without anyone else around. I was happiest there when the grad students just put in an order for some work and I got it done. Alone.

Today I was not so lucky. George was in the animal room with me. I hated George. I was pretty sure he knew this, but it was like he had this thick gauze around his brain that let him experience life at half the volume everyone else was subjected to.

And he wanted to learn.

"You can watch." I said.

He nodded appreciatively and planted himself on a stool beside the fume hood.

Mouse one. Weighed. Responsiveness assessed. Into the CO_2 chamber. I watched carefully as she seemed to come out of her coma of pain to fight against the fumes that were now suffocating her. She tried to move her wasted little body to the side of the chamber but she was just too weak. She gave up in a huff and continued gasping for air that would never come.

"Is she dead?"

I always let the mice have another ten seconds after I noticed they stopped breathing. Just in case.

"Yeah." I pulled off the lid of the chamber and took out the small mouse. She was still warm. I laid her limp body on the dissecting mat and snapped her tiny foot. She didn't flinch. I got my scalpel ready and went to work.

George needed the livers of the mice.

My hands were working on their own. They'd memorized this procedure and now it was automatic. I didn't even have to think about it.

Mouse two. Three. Four. I had ten mice in total. This was just a preliminary experiment, hence the low numbers. Normally I'd be at this for hours.

As I finished with the ninth mouse, George spoke up. I'd almost forgotten he was there.

"Emily? Could I try harvesting the last liver?"

I looked at him like he was insane. I was willing to do this. Mostly because I didn't trust anyone else with them. Why on earth would he want to do this?

"Why?"

He sat up a little straighter and cleared his throat. So gross. "Well, you know, my research is going to involve a lot of *in vivo* work. I guess I just want some experience."

I didn't know what to say. Technically these were his mice. I hated that. "Yeah, it's your experiment."

I tried hard to convey the risk of ruining it all with my tone but I'd forgotten about his mummified brain. He jumped up excitedly and took my stool at the fume hood.

"Wow, this is awkward." he said as he adjusted to working under the glass screen.

"I'd be happy to pull the CO_2 chamber out and let it fill up the room for you." I said.

He actually stopped and thought about it for a moment. "Wouldn't filling the room up with CO_2 be dangerous?"

I sighed. They had safety meetings on this. I'd attended them and seen George there as well. "Very good, George. Now take the lid off the CO_2 chamber and put the mouse in there."

He managed to get the lid off the chamber easily enough but the mouse was another story. She was a control mouse and control mice are always doing better than the ones with the chemotherapy, even though they both had cancer. I knew that if we kept them alive longer, the experimental mice would probably win out but that wasn't the point of this experiment and most others. For this one, George just needed the livers to see how the drug had affected the organ.

The wily mouse scooted around her cage, racing away from the chubby, clumsy fingers that tried to catch her.

"Dammit," he muttered every time she eluded him.

I would have offered to help but I figured that the more difficult I made this, the less inclined George would be to participate the next time I had to do one of his experiments.

Finally, he got her. It was an awkward catch and he all but threw her into the CO_2 chamber. He slammed the lid down and exhaled loudly. He looked at me, all smiles and joy.

"Whoa! You make this look so easy!"

Okay. Bitchy comments repressed. For the moment.

There was a knock at the door. Lynn poked her tiny head in. "Emily?"

Mouse ten was still gasping for air. "What?"

"I'm sorry, I know you're busy but could you tell me where to find that stain I ordered?"

I thought back to that morning's deliveries. Yes, it had come in. "Uh, yeah. I'll grab it for you in a second." I looked back at the mouse. Still breathing.

"Sorry Emily, but I really need it now. I wasn't thinking and I started priming my slides. I need that stain in about two minutes."

"Uh, yeah. Okay. George? Leave her in there until I get back, even if she stops breathing."

George nodded quickly.

I took off my lab coat, washed my hands and headed out the door without bothering to dry them.

"Thanks Emily. I checked where the stains are normally kept but I just couldn't find it," Lynn said apologetically.

"Yeah, that's because it needs to be refrigerated," I said. I hadn't meant to sound like I thought she was an idiot but I know that's exactly how it came out.

"Oh. I didn't know that." she said quietly.

I actually felt bad. Again. Was I suffering from PMS? Why was I suddenly giving a shit about what they thought?

"Yeah, you wouldn't have. The package the stains get shipped in tells me how to store them." I tried to smooth it over without making too big of a deal of it.

"Oh!" she said brightly. "We really should pay a little more attention around here! I totally didn't know that! You just take care of it all. Guess we're really spoiled."

Oh God, just shut up now. I picked up the pace and hurried to the fridge, riffled around a bit and pulled out the tiny bottle.

"Two hundred bucks for twenty-five milliliters. Use it wisely young grasshopper."

She smiled so wide you'd have thought I'd just offered her a kidney.

Must leave now. I damn near ran back to the kill room.

"Sorry about that." I said as I threw open the door.

George snapped his head up and looked like I'd just caught him masturbating. I probably would have screamed less in the end had that been the case. The way he was hunched and his arms hovered in the fume hood made it clear that the fucker had started removing the liver without me.

In two giant steps I was at the fume hood.

"What the fuck are you doing?" I yelled. "I told you to wait!"

I looked in the hood and felt my heart stop. There was blood all over the dissection mat. The tiny mouse was on her back with her guts flayed open. Her tiny forepaws were weakly waving.

"Get out of here!" I shrieked. "You are such a fucking idiot! Get out of here!" I shoved him off the stool and folded the flaps of the mouse's skin back over her stomach. As quickly and gently as I could, I flipped her onto her stomach and put the handle of the scalpel at her neck. My other hand tugged sharply on her tail and then it was done.

Cervical dislocation. Not a pretty procedure, but it was quick and before the mouse even had a chance to be afraid, the lights were out.

I dropped the scalpel and leaned away from the bloody mess in front of me. I don't know how long I watched it. I don't remember when I started sobbing.

"Emily?"

I whirled around at the sound of my name. It was Robert. When had George left?

He looked at the fume hood and then at my hands. His eyes widened and he reached for the nearest drawer. He tore open a box of tissues and shoved a wad against my hand.

"Jesus, Em. You're bleeding pretty bad."

I suddenly felt my palm throbbing. I looked back at the fume hood and saw the scalpel laying there.

"I must have grabbed the blade." My voice was so quiet.

"Jesus! Those buggers are sharp!"

I gently shook my head. "I was on mouse ten. Pretty dull."

He gently pulled away the tissues and nodded. "Yeah, you're probably right. This would've been a lot worse. Still, I think you need some stitches. Why weren't you wearing gloves?"

I came back to myself. "You think that would have made the winning difference?"

He shook his head and smiled. "No. I guess you're right. But you should be wearing gloves with these mice, you know that."

"He was hurting her."

He looked up at me and for a split second, I was sure he could see it all. Like I'd written every horrible memory in thick black letters across my face for him to read. He glanced at the bloody mess in the fume hood and then back at my hand.

"George is an idiot." he said.

I laughed a little. It was that laugh at the end of a good cry that comes along with the overwhelming fatigue of an emotional tornado.

He looked up at me again. This time he smiled. "Let me put these little ladies away. And then I'll take you to the hospital."

"Her liver. I didn't get it yet."

He nodded and slapped on a pair of blue gloves. He crouched beside me, never once asking me for the stool. He flipped the mouse over onto her back again and gently pulled away the ragged flaps of skin. He reached for the scalpel and then shook his head.

"Bastard." he muttered.

"What?"

He folded the flaps of skin closed again and gently placed her in the Ziploc bag with her nine sisters. "He made a mess in there. It's no good."

I closed my eyes and sighed. It's not like this didn't happen all the time. Some mistake along the way made the mouse's forced sacrifice null and void. That was research. Her liver would never be chopped up and tested like the others. She died in a most horrible way for nothing.

Robert cleaned up the rest of the hood without a word. He turned off the CO_2, mopped up the blood, rinsed and dried all the tools, put the preserved livers away and disposed of the now useless mice.

"Come on." he said.

I knew what was coming tonight and I had to save every ounce of my strength to withstand it. I didn't argue with him. He grabbed my bag and my jacket and led me out of the building and to his car. He opened the door for me. I normally would have said something horribly feminist like *I've got two hands, one to get the door and the other to slap you for thinking otherwise,* but that was dumb. I didn't have two hands right now. I didn't even have one. The one was busy bleeding and the other was busy keeping the other one from over doing it.

He didn't try to talk to me on the way to the hospital. I wished he would. So I could hate him for it. As he pulled up to the emergency entrance, I awkwardly gathered my things and tried to elbow the door open.

"Hey, hold on, I'll get it." he said, already out of his seat.

Couldn't he just reach across me and stare down my shirt? Something indecent would have helped my directionless rage at that moment.

"Thanks." I said as I stepped out. "I'll see you tomorrow."

"I can come with you." he offered.

I shook my head. "No, you'd better go. I think George is probably hiding under a rock. You can tell him I bled to death so it's safe to come out now."

He smiled and nodded. "Can I pick you up?"

I shook my head again. "There's a bus that goes right to my place. I'm good." I turned away and then felt myself turn around. Like an idiot. "Hey. Thanks."

He looked up and nodded. "Sure, Em. I'll see you tomorrow."

As I sat in the waiting room with my gob of bloody tissue I realized that that punk had started calling me *Em* again. I tried to conjure up some rage for this clear violation of my rules but it just wouldn't boil. I couldn't even get it to simmer.

I tried not to think about sleeping that night. I knew exactly what was coming. Julia would visit me that night. She'd replay the saddest day of my life. I wish I could have gone to Creekside or back to the lab. Neither were great options at the moment considering how fantastically unstable I had just revealed myself to be. Sure I'd been an absolute cunt to people but never like this. Never so emotional, so out of control. Not in a really long time. The threads holding me together were fraying a little more every day.

The Black Box

There she was. My little baby sister. Dead.

I knelt down beside the tub. The bloody water had spilled over onto the yellow linoleum floor and it was soaking into my jeans. It was warm.

I didn't even think as I reached for the faucet and turned the water off. I reached up to her beautiful, childlike face. I brushed her matted bangs away from her forehead. Her large blue eyes stared at the ceiling. They were empty. They looked like glass.

I touched her lips. Her cheeks. Her nose. She was still so beautiful.

The tears hovered on my eyelids and blurred my vision. I brushed them away angrily. I needed to see her.

Her body floated easily in the bath. Her round breasts, far too much of a burden for any fifteen year old, broke the surface of the red water. She had twisted herself to fit all in the tub and one long, white thigh stretched above the water.

I don't know when my aunt got home. I don't remember hearing her scream and scream. I don't remember the police breaking down our door. I don't remember any of it.

Julia had been pregnant. I remember being told that. The autopsy showed that she had been six weeks along. I wanted to run away. I wanted to vomit. I wanted to scream. I wanted to drive straight into a telephone pole. Anything but this. Anything but missing her.

I settled on burning Mr. Greene's house to the ground.

As I watched it burn, I realized that I wanted to be caught. I pictured it perfectly. As they dragged me away to be locked up, I would scream endlessly about Mr. Greene's part in my sister's death. How he might as well of handed her the razor blade the first time he told her he loved her.

Dumb Emily might have made that happen for me but she had not been at the wheel that night. Mr. Greene's house was a big, cheap looking stucco mansion set up in the outskirts of town. No one was close by. As I doused the front porch in gasoline, I screamed and shrieked as if I had gone completing insane. I threw rocks at the windows, hoping that the breaking glass would help me somehow. It didn't.

I knew there was an out of town game. Mr. Greene would be there, cheering on his troop of chumps across the basketball court. Mrs. Greene would also be there, smiling proudly, pointing out *Daddy* to her son.

Daddy. Mr. Greene and I would have been related.

I thought the fire would make me feel better. I guess in a sense it did but not in the way I had been expecting. As the fire licked through the house, invading every bit of their home, I felt like it was going through me too. It was like the flames were eating up every memory of Julia, every feeling of Julia and turning it to ash. A heart made of ash didn't work as well as the one being burned within me, but it also didn't hurt. It didn't feel anything.

The world took on a washed out appearance after that night. My friends never existed, my dreams turned to dust. There was this empty husk of an Emily left behind. People think that killing yourself is the only way to give up. I probably once agreed with them. I know now that this is not true. There are so many ways to give up.

But even though the engines failed and I nosed dived into an existence void of emotion, a black box survived. And that's where my beautiful Julia waited. This black box was indestructible. The only thing I could do to keep the memory of my baby sister from trying to paste together the ashes of my broken and burned heart was to bury the black box I had hidden her away in.

Hasenpfeffer

I woke up the next morning on the floor of Julia's room. I felt hung-over and my hand hurt. It took me a moment to realize that I felt hung-over because I was. An empty bottle of cheap wine was just out of my reach. And it took an even longer moment to remember what I had done to my hand. It wasn't all a bad dream. It was all real.

I stood up too quickly and had to sit right back down on Julia's bed. When my head stopped throbbing I staggered off to my room and picked up my cell to use the only number I had listed in my contacts. *The Lab.*

"Hello?" a friendly voice greeted me.

"Hey, it's Emily. I'm not coming in today. Bye." I hung up.

I brushed my teeth, washed down a few painkillers with some lukewarm water and went back to sleep, but this time in a bed.

I didn't wake up again until five in the evening and only did so because my cell phone rang. The sound was alien to me because it rang so infrequently.

"Hello?"

"Hi, Em?" This was not my boss.

"Yeah, who's this?"

"Hey, it's Robert. I wanted to see how you're doing, and I was hoping I could come by your place this afternoon to drop off some get well flowers George got you."

I sat up. My headache roared back to life with my sudden movement but my heart was beating faster now and my stomach felt like it was full of helium.

"Uh, wow, that's really nice of you."

"It's no problem! I'm not doing anything tonight anyways. Where do you live?"

"Hey, thanks but don't worry about it. I'll be back in the lab tomorrow, I'm sure the flowers will keep." My words seemed to clunk out, one at a time.

"It's Saturday tomorrow. Really, I'd like to see you." He was asking now, not offering.

I felt my throat tighten as a familiar presence took hold. Dumb Emily shoved my pathetic self aside and answered for me. "Okay, sounds good. But I've been inside all day and I'm feeling a lot better. How about we get that dinner we missed. I'll try to stay for the actual eating part."

He laughed. "Yeah! That'd be great! I'll come get you, okay?"

"Sure, call when you get here, I'm at 756 Oak Street. I'll come down. No where fancy though, kay? I've got enough focus to find my jeans and that's about it."

"I'll be there soon." And he hung up.

The music was just as trendy as the servers. Stylish coifs and fashion forward clothes spiced up otherwise plain human beings. I'd never been here before.

A girl with a partially shaved head and pink streaks sat us at a table near the window and took our drink order.

"I'm really glad you feel better," Robert said.

"I was hung-over."

He sat up a little straighter but he smiled. "Really?"

"Not in the good, frat house way. How'd things go at the lab today?"

He shrugged. "We managed. But just barely. An order came in for Shirley and George signed for it and left it on the counter. Turns out it was tissue samples and they weren't packed properly."

I groaned. He didn't even have to say it. "Wasted?"

He nodded. "Yeah, Shirley missed you."

I scoffed. "Yeah, she missed me as in this is the one fucking day that I actually need Emily and she gets sick! What a little bitch!"

Much to my surprise, Robert laughed. "Wow, that was perfect! That's actually exactly what she said! I wasn't going to say anything but I guess you're watching us enough to already know what we'd say anyways."

I couldn't help myself and I smiled. "Those were nice flowers. Is George okay?"

"Yeah, he's fine. Feels pretty bad though. " He looked at me.

My stomach dropped and my throat tightened. I silently willed him to keep his questions to himself.

In some strange way, my silent request manifested itself. The server came up to our table and dropped off our drinks. Robert had ordered a beer and I had a glass of tomato juice. I didn't drink often and an entire bottle of Jude's bargain red was not treating me kindly. Robert sat up straighter as the server rearranged our table to fit the coasters and the drinks. Just then I noticed how much crap was on this table. Salt and pepper shakers, two candle holders, a small statuette of the Virgin Mary and some fake flowers in a cheap plastic vase.

"You ready to order?"

Robert looked at me and raised his eyebrows. "Em, you want some more time?"

"Uh, tell her what you want. I'll know by then." I scrambled to grab the long, awkward menu. I scanned the tiny, strange print for something I recognized. The truth was that I didn't care what I ate.

"I'll get this pasta." Robert said, pointing out his choice to the server.

"Oh that is so good!" the server gushed. "And you?"

"Yeah, uh, can I get soup?"

"We don't serve soup. We have Hasenpfeffer, wanna try it?"

"Sure, thanks." I shoved the menu at her.

Robert was smiling like he knew something I didn't.

"What?"

"I just didn't think you'd be into rabbit is all."

"What the fuck are you talking about?"

He laughed. "Hasenpfeffer. It's rabbit."

"I ask for soup and the bitch recommends rabbit?" I was shrieking now. "What kind of place is this? No soup, here, have some bunny instead?"

Robert laughed again. "It's stew!"

I looked down at my bandaged hand and muttered a few choice words to myself.

Robert stopped laughing. "Em? You okay?"

"Yup! Good!" I searched the restaurant for the blaze of pink streaks and made a desperate wave for the waitress. I caught her eye and pointed to Robert's glass and then to me. I wasn't making it through dinner without more alcohol. She smiled and gave me the thumbs up. "Sorry, I know that is so rude."

"What's that?"

"Waving the waitress down like she's a bus."

Robert smiled again. "It's okay, I'll leave her a good tip."

I nodded and looked back down at my hand. I hadn't been out for a dinner with anyone since the attempt at sushi with Robert and before that, it had been a very long time. I didn't know what to say to people anymore unless they were dead, or potential figments of my fragile psyche, or I was trying to get rid of them. Robert was real and quite alive. And I didn't want him to go anywhere.

"So...how was your trip?" Good, I thought. That's something people ask other people.

He looked at me like I had a second head and then recognition set in. "Oh the conference! Yeah, that was alright. The boss doesn't know how you knew about his IBS but he was grateful for your strategic seating arrangements. Next time though, he'd like first class as well if possible."

A choked laugh escaped me. "I'll keep that in mind. Honestly I had no idea about his little gut condition. I was just annoyed that he asked me to book the tickets. Hope you liked yours."

"That was the best part of the trip actually. Thanks. Those conferences are just...." He trailed off.

"Why do you go?"

He shrugged his shoulders. "It's a good way to make contacts. And it's how it's played." He looked at me and smiled. I felt like an ant under a microscope.

Once again, the pink haired waitress saved me and dropped off my beer. "I know what that's like! Can't stand to be the only sober one at a table." she said.

"Thanks." I grabbed the cold glass and drank deeply from it. Oh hell, I pounded it back. As I set the empty glass down, my eyes went back to my hand. "I'm not an alcoholic. Drinking is just convenient at this point in time."

I waited for the sound of his chair pulling out and footsteps leaving the table. That would have been okay. I was here, present, but so were the table and chairs. The floor, the salt and pepper shakers. We were all here, watching the truly alive world go on without us and that was okay. Except he didn't leave.

I looked up just as he was setting down his own glass of beer. It was empty. "I might be taking a cab home if we keep this up."

"Rabbit stew is pretty good." I said as we stepped out of the restaurant.

Robert stopped walking and bent over. I thought he was going to throw up but he was actually laughing uncontrollably.

"It...looked like vomit," he managed between fits of giggles.

"Hey, fuck you. Yours looked like dog shit."

He continued to laugh as we stumbled along the sidewalk towards his car.

"Hey, you're calling a cab, right?"

He nodded as he dug through his pockets for his keys. "Yeah. But I'll drive you home first."

What? I actually had to stop for a second and think about what he had just said. "Don't be a fucking idiot. I'd rather walk."

He looked at me like I'd just asked him to find a derivative or something. And then it dawned on him. "Oh, right! That doesn't make any sense at all."

"Good to see you can hold your liquor."

I'd lost count at four beers and we were both well past the point of functionally drunk. I felt like I was on a little rowboat at sea but I still had the good sense to take a cab home. Having your mother driven into a telephone pole by a drunk driver kind of burns that particular rule of modern society into your brain.

"I'm fine. I'm good to go."

"Come on, don't be an asshole. Gimme your keys." I held out my hand and could tell that it was swaying a bit.

He smiled like a complete goof. "What will you give me for them?"

I sighed. And then lifted my shirt up. The look on his face was something else. I grabbed the keys out of his hand during his momentary stupor but he didn't fight it.

"I don't have any numbers for cabs on hand, do you?"

He nodded and pulled out his phone like he was in a trance. I could only hope he had called the right number because he asked for two cabs to the corner of Breast and Samson. We were at Rest and Samson but close enough. I'm sure the cabbies could decipher it.

"Em? I'm going to kiss you now."

He stood in front of me and sloppily pushed me up against his car. We both smelled like beer and neither of us had particularly good coordination. He groped me as if he was messing around with *PlayDo*. My head was swimming and each move was another dangerous heave of the sea I found myself in.

"I'm gonna be sick!" I pushed him off of me and ran to the back of his car. The frothy acid, beer and rabbit stew covered the ground at my feet.

"Em? Em? Are you okay?"

"Fuck off, I'm fine." I said between my gasps for air and spits of whatever was still in my mouth.

I stood up and took a deep breath of night air. The imaginary sea had calmed.

Robert came up beside me and looked down at my feet. "See? I told you the rabbit stew looked like vomit."

Gifts come in Plastic Baggies

I went into Julia's room and found her dusty collection of board games. Scrabble, Yahtzee and Trivial Pursuit were all coming with me. I grabbed one of the many decks of cards that Jude picked up at casinos and headed out the door.

The day was bright and the sky was blue. It was one of those days that was impossible to waste because no matter where you were, it was beautiful.

As I made the long trek to Creekside, my thoughts wandered back to dinner. Rabbit stew is surprisingly good and Robert had been...perfect. He didn't ask me anything I couldn't answer. By the end of the night I had felt myself wanting him to ask. Ask me why I wasn't a grad student, ask me why I had flipped out in the lab, ask me why I was always alone. But he didn't. The seams that held together my fragile disguise were breaking down, thread by thread, and he had been good enough not to mention it.

The little hospital in the forest clearing looked like an island in the middle of a sea, just begging to be overtaken. I wondered how long it could possibly sit there, forgotten.

I didn't have to see him to know that Angus was outside of the white room. A cloud of blue smoke billowed out from the room that served to hide their strange corner of the universe.

"Hey cowboy. How's it going?"

He barely shrugged. "Not bad. A couple of kids came through here last night, smoking dope and getting mighty happy about their lot in life. They discussed some interesting things. It was almost better than TV." Each word had an effortless way about it. Any one of his words completely carried his swagger and ease and I-could-give-a-shit attitude. I'd never met anyone like him and my awe of this long gone man was renewed every time I saw him.

"Yeah, I bet. I brought some stuff for you guys. I figured you might be getting bored of eating so I brought a deck of cards and some board games. I don't know, I think they're boring as shit but then again a couple of marbles and bottle caps would spice this place up, so you know..."

No approval. Or disapproval. He just took another long drag of his cigarette.

"How you doing for those?" I asked.

"Supply is holding steady, thank you." He gently butted out the cigarette and lovingly tucked it away. "Shall we?"

I nodded.

Angus stood in front of the wall but nothing happened. I was about to ask if something was wrong when he turned back to me. "Emily, why'd you want to know?"

"What?"

"About us. You said you wanted to know about how we died, see if you could find a pattern. Why would you want to know something like that?"

I hadn't expected that. "I...uh...was just curious. I mean, how many times in a life do you run into this sort of shit! I wanted to know just because."

He looked at me like I was full of shit. Because I was. He turned back to the wall without a word and suddenly it began to peel away.

It hit me the second I looked at them. Doug and Francine were different. They seemed brighter. Like actually brighter. It was like wearing some funny pair of glasses that bent the light about them.

How they acted was different too, but that could have just been in contrast to the moping of Dolly. She snivelled as I told her I hadn't found anything yet.

"It's okay, guess I just wasn't meant to know."

I couldn't believe that I was falling for this. "Hey, I'll keep looking. They were easy to find out about because they died so much more recently."

She sighed and nodded glumly.

I couldn't help but agree with her. Something had changed for Francine and Doug, something good. Knowing had made them happy somehow.

Even talking to them was better. I don't know how long I had been sitting there and I would have continued to if it weren't for Angus.

"I was just outside, Em. It's getting dark so unless you want to bunk out here I suggest you get a move on," he said.

I nodded and stood up from their white table. "See you guys later. Hey, Dolly? I promise I'll keep looking."

Dolly did her best impression of putting on a brave front and smiled.

Angus already had the wall open for me and was waiting.

"Can't wait to see me go, eh?"

He shrugged.

"Hey, don't forget, you invited me in here," I said.

His face softened a little and he nodded. "Yep, that I did."

My hands were shoved into my pockets as I stepped through the wall. Made the cold tingling less creepy. My fingers curled around something plastic and crunchy. I stepped back into the white room and pulled it out. I couldn't help but start laughing.

"What's that you got there?" Angus asked.

"Here." I put it in his hand. "Have fun with these. Let me know if you want some more, I've got a man in the know."

I jumped through the wall and turned just in time to see Angus open the clear plastic baggie and take a big whiff of the two joints I had bought nearly a week ago.

"That was dope, wasn't it?"

It was Sunday and Angus was waiting for me outside the white room.

"Yeah, thought you might want to give it a try. Liven things up."

He chuckled. "Is that supposed to be a joke?"

I thought about what I had just said and saw the pun. I hated puns. "No, I...whatever. How was it?"

"It was interesting to say the least. Ready to come in?" He was already putting his cigarette away.

"Yeah. How's Dolly doing?"

Angus sighed. "About as good as yesterday. I wish you'd hurry up and find something."

"It's not like I haven't been looking! Christ, it's not just a matter of running to city hall."

"You found out about Franny and Doug easy enough." he shot back.

"Yeah, they haven't been dead for thirty years! I'm looking, okay? What's it to you anyway? You didn't want to me to even dig in the first place?"

He was about to say something when it caught at the back of his throat. I could see him swallow the words. "Come on, I'm sure they're just dying to see you."

"Oh fuck off, Angus."

He stopped just short of the wall and turned back to me. If I'd ever had a dad around to piss off to the point of considering beating my ass, I'm pretty sure he would've had the same look Angus had now.

But the cowboy played it cool. He turned away from me and my lame attempt at insulting him.

I considered just leaving, but through the open wall I could see Francine and Doug shuffling about happily and Dolly slumped at their little white table.

"Hey guys, how's it going?"

Francine turned to me and beamed. She looked different again. Like she was thinner and happier. "Emily! Come on over and have a sit beside me! What's new since yesterday?"

I couldn't help but smile back at her. "Not much, Francine. You look...amazing."

She smiled brightly. "Yeah, I don't know what the hell's going on but I feel great. Like it's all starting again."

Doug took a chair across from me and he looked like he had grown younger by about ten years. "Wow, Doug. You look...thin."

He chuckled and held up the deck of cards I had brought them yesterday. "Poker?"

I nodded. Dolly was slumped beside me and had been whimpering since I sat down.

"Hey, Dolly. You want to play?"

She buried her face in her folded arms and sobbed *no*.

"Dolly, I'm still looking. Honestly. We'll find something, even if I have to go to Las Vegas myself and dig you up. I'll figure it out."

She peeked out from her arms. Her eyes were red and watery. "Really?"

"Yeah, really. Look, maybe you can help me out. Is there anything you remember? Like, what club were you working at, any friends you had. Anything?"

Her big doll eyes looked thoughtfully at her hands as she kneaded them together awkwardly. "Big Jimmie was my boss. Tula Bing was the bartender. But for the life of me I can't remember anything else!" She was going to start sobbing again.

"That's really helpful. Don't worry, I'll figure it out. You don't remember the name of the club do you?"

"Yeah, it was just called Big Jimmie's. Kind of a dive but I was working my way up to one of the big casinos." This distant memory of her ambition seemed to perk her up a bit.

"Okay, that really helps Dolly."

She smiled brightly and wiped away her tears. If she'd been made of something other than...soul, her heavy makeup would have smeared right off.

After one game, I decided to leave. Doug and Francine were easy to be around but Angus was like a shadow that kept moving out of the corner of my eye and Dolly was just miserable. Plus, I didn't really understand Texas Hold 'em anyways. "Hey, I know I haven't been here long but I should go. It was starting to get dark when I got here and I don't want to be creeping through the woods at night." I said.

Angus walked me to the wall and stepped out with me. "That's a big hunk of bullshit you fed me the other day about you just being curious. Cats are curious. Snot nosed kids are curious, and you ain't either."

"Look, I just wanted to know. Doesn't look like Francine and Doug really minded that much finding out the truth." My voice came out stronger than I had expected. I didn't like talking about Julia, not to anyone, and Angus was pushing me dangerously close to doing it.

"No, I suppose you're right. They don't seem to mind one bit." he answered cautiously.

"I'll come back tomorrow. Any special orders?"

He shook his head. "No, we don't need anything."

I couldn't help but feel as though what he really just said was that *We don't need you.*

Jude was asleep as usual when I got home. The television set was blaring about some new ridiculous blanket that fits like a robe.

"Then just buy a fucking robe." I muttered to myself as I turned off the TV.

Mr. Puggums protested weakly from my aunt's lap.

"You weren't watching that anyways, Puggums," I said as I scratched his bony back. He purred like a bunch of pennies rattling around an old tin can.

The cat got up and jumped down from my aunt's lap. She shivered from the sudden loss of heat when I noticed that the living room window was wide open. I closed that and threw an old blanket over my aunt before returning to my room. Mr. Puggums followed me in.

I looked at my sleeping computer for a minute before finally turning it on. Angus's sharp disapproval of what I was doing had given my brain something to gnaw at and feel bad about.

I wanted to know how they died so I could have some idea about where Julia might be. I wasn't religious in the slightest but I couldn't shy away from the idea that maybe some higher being had decided that Julia had really fucked up and was now punishing her for it. I mean, if Angus and the others were right and that white room was purgatory, and Julia was in a room like that somewhere...

Then what?

I had no clue how I'd found the Creekside spooks. I couldn't possibly stumble upon Julia and even if I did what could I even do for her? Bring her grape slushies and penny candies?

My computer finally beeped to life. It was old but it still ran and I was not a material person as of late. It wasn't like I didn't want a new computer or nicer clothes, I just really didn't even think about it.

Big Jimmie's, Las Vegas. With the speed of light Google got me more than I needed. There were ten listings for *Big Jimmie's* in Las Vegas alone.

"Get some fucking originality," I muttered to myself. I pulled out a notepad and my cell. I didn't know what to ask but there was nowhere else to start except *hi, anyone remember Dolly?*

The first number rang and rang. The second was answered by a woman with a nasal voice and a thick Jersey lick to her words. She hadn't heard of Moira or Dolly. Same thing with the next two numbers. The fifth number had no one who spoke English on the other end, the sixth and seventh were disconnected, the eighth and ninth didn't have anyone around that recognized the name and the tenth was a pizza joint. I knew it was a long shot. The place she'd worked at was probably a *Starbucks* by now.

I'd been on the phone for about forty minutes already. In research you get used to getting nowhere fast but I was a little pissed about my lack of progress here. I paced around my room for a few minutes before I noticed that my phone was blinking. I had a message waiting.

It was Robert. My stomach dropped as I listened to his awkward message. He wanted to hang out if I wasn't busy. I was already dialling him back before I had decided what to say.

"Emily!"

My brain ran through the pitch and tempo of my name and tried to glean some hidden message from it all. Was he surprised I called? Maybe even happy?

"I'm glad you got my message. I'm just sitting around and wanted to know if you were up for hanging out. We could go see a movie?" His invitation hung out there, vulnerable.

"Uh, yeah. That'd be great. Which movie did you have in mind?"

"I don't know. Uh, I can come get you and maybe while I'm on my way over you could have a look through the listings?"

Normally I would have berated him for this. Why would he suggest going to the movies if he didn't have one in mind. But then I realized that normally I wouldn't even have said yes.

"Sure, call me when you're downstairs."

"Great! I'll see you in a bit."

I just let Dumb Emily have this one. I wanted to see Robert again.

"There's really nothing playing at all," I said as I slid into the front seat.

"Oh. We could just get some coffee then?"

"Yeah, sure. That sounds good. There's a coffee shop just over on sixth."

"Oh yeah, I like that one."

I hated it. But I hated most things. "Hey, I've actually been inside most of the day." Lie. "Would you mind if we got the coffee to go?"

"Sure, sounds good. Where'd you want to go? It's pretty warm tonight, we could go down to the beach?"

"Yeah. That'd be kind of perfect actually."

He looked at me and smiled. I felt my mouth attempt an awkward twist of its own but I'm sure I just looked insane.

Huntsville was on an inlet. The sea air without the open winds felt amazing. I hadn't been down to the beach in years.

We hopped along the rocky shore until we came to a small clearing of perfect, soft sand. It wasn't even wet. I hadn't noticed but Robert had tucked a blanket under his arm. He laid it out and emptied his pockets.

"What's all this?" I said as I kneeled down beside him. Tiny candy bars and mini-packs of licorice and jujubes were scattered across the blanket.

"I thought we were going to the movies. I never like what they have there."

In spite of myself, I was liking Robert more and more.

"And the blanket?"

He looked at me for a second like I had said something that didn't quite make sense and then his eyes got wide. "No! Oh, Em, I didn't....no, that's not why I brought it, I swear!"

I smiled at him and it came easily. "I'm just giving you a hard time."

He seemed to calm down and ease a little. "Finally get you to hang out with me and I make you think I'm some sort of pervert."

"Why would wanting to have sex with me make you a pervert?"

He stopped short of answering.

Now it was my turn to backtrack. "I mean, I'm not saying you do or anything, just that if you did it wouldn't make you sick."

"I do."

"What?"

"I do want you, but that's not why I brought the blanket." He looked off to the side as he said it.

"Oh." I didn't think about the words before they came out. "I want you too."

He snapped his head towards me. I could hear him breathing and my own heart thumping. My head was light and all I could do to keep from passing out was to anchor myself to him. I pulled him towards me and clumsily kissed him. I didn't know what I was doing but between the two of us a rhythm was found and all the awkward moments were gone. Under the piles of ill fitting sweaters and ugly shirts was a smooth, hard chest and a pair of strong arms that wrapped around me. As if we'd never get another chance at it, our hands ran over each other's bodies, learning the curves and angles of one another.

"I'm already in love with you, Emily." he whispered.

Tula Bing

I was exhausted when I got home the next morning. But good exhausted. I felt like I had drunk too much but it had been worth it. I don't know why I did what I did but it didn't matter right then. I crawled into bed and slept until noon.

I thought about going in to work for a half day and then decided against it. Instead, I called in sick unapologetically and then got on my computer and tackled the mystery of Dolly's demise from a different angle. *Listings for Tula Bing, Las Vegas.* Despite this being one of the most unusual names I had ever heard, Google still found me four listings.

I got to it right away. The first three were all escorts that were severely pissed that someone named Dolly was passing their name around. I tried to explain to the first that Dolly had just named Tula as a friend, that I wasn't sure if this was the right Tula, but that sent her off the deep end.

"What? There's more than one Tula Bing? Those bitches are probably stealing all my clients!"

I hung up. With the next two I just didn't even bother getting that far.

The fourth was something different.

"No, Tula's my grandma. She doesn't live here anymore."

"Oh. You don't know where I could get in touch with her, do you?"

"Yeah, sure. She's at the Springs old folks home. Want the number?"

"That would be great."

After three nurses, one doctor and the janitor, somehow I had gotten a resident of the Springs Retirement Center on the phone.

"Hi, Ms. Bing?"

"Who?"

"Tula Bing?" I was almost shouting now.

"What? Tula? That's my roommate."

Fuck. "Oh. Could I speak to her please?"

"What?"

"Could you go and get her? I really need to talk to her!"

"Oh, you want to talk to Tula? Why the hell did these idiots give me the phone?"

"I don't know. Sorry."

"What? Sorry? Oh don't be sorry, there's a bunch of useless tits running the show around here. Hold on a sec."

I heard some muffling and after a few long minutes another person got on the phone.

The voice was raspy and hard. It twisted *hello* into something almost frightening.

"Hi, Tula Bing?"

"Yeah, who's this?" This woman had rough edges all around. I wondered if she let her grandchildren call her *Nana*.

"Hi, my name's Emily. My mom was friends with someone I think you used to work with. I'm just trying to track her down."

"Oh yeah, what's your mom's name?"

What had I told Francine's brother? "Doreen Simmons. She said her friend's name was Moira Seeley but most people called her Dolly." Whoever Doreen was, I was going to have to send her flowers and an apology note for pretending that she was my mother on now two occasions.

The other end of the line was quiet. I was about to say something when Tula's raspy voice made me stop short.

"Are you a cop or something? Trying to make a name for yourself?"

"What? No, I really just want to find Dolly."

"Hmph. Well, some friend your mother is. Dolly's dead. She's been dead for years."

"Oh. She said they lost touch after Dolly left Jersey."

"Yeah, Las Vegas will do that to people."

"Ms. Bing, when did she die?"

Tula sighed heavily. "I don't really know. She's been on the missing persons list since the seventies. And if you are full of shit and really are a cop, you put down that I told those bastards what I knew had happened to her, but that they didn't do shit about it."

My stomach clenched like a fist. "What are you talking about?"

"Dolly was picked up for her last gig at Big Jimmie's. A retirement party for a bunch of cops. She was moving over to the *Riviera* after that. Even stole her new costume for her last gig at Jimmie's." She laughed. "Oh Jesus help us, that girl felt like a princess in that little red and blue jumpsuit. Not once did it get into that thick head of hers that she looked like a streetwalker. I told that son-of-a-bitch that sending his girls out like that was dangerous. He didn't give a shit about any of them and Dolly, well...if your mom was any friend of hers she'd know that as sweet as that kid was, she was dumber than a sack of shit."

"She was murdered?"

"Never saw her again but there ain't no other explanation. Brute cops got too drunk and messed around with her. Not like she'd be the first girl to go missing in Las Vegas. I tried to tell the cops in charge of her case what I knew but they didn't want to hear it of their own. Got my windshield smashed in and my tires slashed. All sorts of crank calls telling me to keep my mouth shut. Would've gone out there and found Dolly myself but I had a kid. I couldn't be doing that."

"She was never found?"

"No. But it doesn't take a genius to figure it all out, especially after seeing the guilty looks down at the station."

"I'm really sorry to hear that. I don't know if I should even tell my mom that. She's pretty old."

"Who'd want to know that kind of shit? Nah, I think you've got it right. Tell her Dolly got appendicitis or something classy like that."

"Yeah, I just might do that. Thanks, Ms. Bing."

"Sure. Guess it's nice to know that someone is still thinking about that sweet girl besides me."

And she hung up.

I felt sick. If I had thought for one second that this was even a possibility, I wouldn't have asked to take this on in the first place. Now I was stuck with this and I didn't know what to do with it. How could I tell Dolly this? *Nobody except the bartender gave a crap.*

This was too much too soon. I had been alone and safe for so long but now I felt alive. It was terrifying.

My backpack was full of new magazines and junk food as I headed off to the forest. I walked past Shirley from the lab but she took one look at me and kept on walking. Guess she was still pissed about her rotten tissue samples.

I wondered if she would tattle on me. *Go ahead, tell my crappy boss that I'm not actually dying*, I thought.

And then I wondered if Robert had made it to the lab that day. The thought of him made me smile like an idiot.

The day was bright and sunny and that helped a little. I still hadn't decided what to say to Dolly but I felt myself definitely leaning one way.

Angus was waiting outside.

"Hey, how'd you know I'd be here at this time?"

He chuckled. "You think I've got anything better to do than wait out here for you? Besides, it's just odd in there. Dolly moping about and Francine and Doug looking more like angels every day."

"What?"

"Well, like you said, they didn't seem to mind knowing. It's changed them. They're...lighter. For the love of God, tell me you found something for Dolly. That woman has been shaken with a serious case of the blues. I don't know what to do for her."

"Yeah, I did." The reluctance in my voice was clear. I couldn't hide it.

His eyes widened. "Is it bad?"

I nodded. "I don't know what to do, Angus."

He took a drag from his cigarette and thought for a long moment. "You'll know. For some reason you found us, so I know you'll do the right thing."

"Yeah, right."

"A little bit of advice? Honesty isn't always the best policy. Anyone that says different is full of shit or has alienated everyone with the truth."

I looked up at him as he tucked his cigarette away. "What if the truth is the point? What if that's what made Francine and Doug the way they are now?"

"Well, the way I see it is that if Dolly doesn't get out of this funk she's in from you telling her something nice, you can always tell her the truth later on. I never believed that truth telling was a one shot deal."

I nodded and we went inside.

Francine and Doug did look lighter and the change from yesterday was noticeable. Dolly looked horrible.

"Hey, that information you gave me really panned out."

Her big eyes got unbelievably bigger. "Really? So how'd it happen?"

I looked over at Angus and picked up on the faintest of nods.

"Appendicitis. You had gotten a job at the *Riviera* and didn't want to miss your first shift. Tula said you did really well even though you were dancing through your appendix bursting. By the time you took a rest it was too late."

Dolly gasped and put a hand over her mouth. "I got hired at the *Riviera?*"

Of course that's what she would fixate on. "Yeah, you did. That's their old costume." I said, pointing at her ridiculous outfit.

"Appendicitis? Is that bad?"

"Yeah, pretty bad."

"Well golly gee. Guess I was just too excited to notice!"

94

I stayed for a while and didn't notice any changes in Dolly like I had in Doug and Francine, but she was definitely happier. Even Francine listened to her gush about how she'd made it.

Angus stepped out of the room with me and breathed in the musty air of the old hospital.

"Well, Dolly seems pretty happy." he said.

"Yeah, I think so. I hope it worked."

He looked at me. "So that wasn't the whole truth?"

I shook my head. "She did actually get hired on at the *Riviera.*"

He nodded and looked away. "Probably for the best. You've got some crocodile skin on you and if it made you a little green thinking about how she died then I'm thinking it might have made Dolly pass out."

"Yeah, I think so too. It was pretty bad."

He didn't ask and I respected that. What good would it do him to know?

"Okay, well I should go before it gets too dark." I turned to leave.

"Emily?"

"Yeah?"

"Who'd you lose?"

My stomach knotted up. "What do you mean?"

He took a step towards me. "I mean that you found four spooks living in a wall. You got to know us and decided to do some investigation. Why? Why are you so comfortable with us? With all this..."

"Death?"

"Well, yeah."

He waited. I didn't know what to say so the truth came out. But just a little.

"I lost my mom when I was twenty and then my sister died when I was twenty-four. I guess I am a little too used to this."

Angus nodded. "Yeah, that's a bit much I suppose. Least you still got your old man around, huh?"

A surprised laugh escaped me. "Yeah, I guess you could say that. Look, I really gotta go."

"Alright now. We'll see you tomorrow?"
"Yeah, I'll try."
No. Don't think I'd try.

Hold My Hand

I was standing in line when someone took my hand. I was so surprised that I didn't pull away immediately. It was Robert.

I untangled my hand from his and looked back at the counter ahead of me.

"Sorry." he mumbled.

I looked over at him. His eyes were downcast.

"Hey, I just...we work together, Robert."

I had just hurt him. Without really even trying.

"It's okay. I'll see you around." And he left.

I was at the front of the line for Nancy's coffee stand. She was gunning me down.

"What you want?" she squawked.

"A latte."

She pounded the cash registers keys until it spit out an arbitrary four dollar and twenty one cent total.

"Hey, Nancy, what does Robert usually get?"

I set the hot chocolate with extra whipped cream down beside him.

"Look Robert, I'm sorry."

He looked up at me and nodded. "Yeah, it's okay."

He wasn't okay.

"I've got a lot to get done after missing work yesterday. I'd better get to it. Thanks for the coffee." he said.

I left his office with the peace offering not having done much besides lighten my wallet.

I sat at my desk all day and barely did anything. No one talked to me, which I was normally okay with. Today I just felt alone.

It was six days before I went back to Creekside. Robert had politely avoided me all week and by Sunday I was craving talking to someone besides Mr. Puggums.

I filled my bag with candies, drinks and other disgusting snacks that living people really shouldn't eat anyways. I grabbed a newspaper for Doug and a couple weekly gossip magazines for Francine and Dolly.

My stomach cramped up as I made my way to the old hospital. I didn't know what to expect of Dolly. Had my lie done more harm than good?

Angus wasn't waiting there when I arrived. I thought about leaving but then I realized the sad truth that I had nowhere to go and no one to be with. I'd made sure of that.

I sat down on one of the old beds. It sagged dangerously. I was sure it was going to give but despite the protesting of the rusted springs, it held me. I grabbed a pop from my bag and one of the magazines. I checked my cell phone at least five times in ten minutes before a strangely interesting article about conjoined twins took my attention from it.

"Well, hello there."

Angus stood a few feet away. How long had I been reading? The day's light was fading and I was long done that first article.

"Hey. How long have you been there? I didn't hear you at all."

He smiled. "Maybe your thoughts were just buzzing too loudly."

He was probably right. When I had first found this place, there was nothing in my life to think about. Now there wasn't just something. There was someone. And I had already hurt him.

"Hey now, what's the matter?"

I suddenly realized I had almost started crying. "Nothing. I brought the paper and some magazines, a few snacks." I grabbed my bag and stood up.

Angus smiled. "You don't have to bring us anything. Just come by."

"Yeah, well, too late."

He waited for me to go through the open wall first before following in behind me. I didn't know what to expect of Dolly and if I was honest about it, I hadn't been expecting, or even hoping for the best, but it came along anyways.

"Emily! You sugar pie! Come on over and play a game of Scrabble with us!" Dolly said happily. She was beaming.

My breath caught in my throat. "Dolly, you look so...happy."

"Well yessir, it's some kind of magic what you did for us. Everything just feels a whole lot better now."

I looked over at Angus. The contrast between him and the others was shocking. It was like they all walked around in their own spotlights and he just stood back in the shadows.

I played a game of Scrabble with them and won despite being accused of making up six words. It was nice being around them again. Being around anybody.

"Alright, I think it's time I got going. I'll try to come by again soon. Any requests?"

"Chocolate cake!" Dolly nearly jumped out of her seat. "Oh, I love chocolate cake, but I hadn't had none since my twelfth birthday. Had to keep the figure trim, you know! Don't really matter now!"

I couldn't stop myself from smiling. "Yeah, you're probably right. Okay, I'll find some. See you later guys."

Angus came over to the wall with me. He got in close like he had some secret to tell. "Em? You know that stuff you gave me? The dope?"

"Yeah, Angus. Giving up on your cigarettes for some herb?"

He chuckled. "No, no. It's just that it seems like kind of a social drug to me. Want to smoke the other one with me?"

I laughed suddenly. "What? Seriously? Now?"

"Well, sure. If it's not too dark out."

I just looked at him. First time I'd ever actually considered smoking weed was with a geriatric spirit stuck in purgatory. Figures, I always had to do things the hard way. Or at least the strange way. "Okay, yeah. Let's try it out," I said. I couldn't wipe the smile off my face.

Angus followed me out of the room and we each took a seat on the closest rusty bed. Angus pulled the plastic baggie out of his pocket and the revolver lighter from his other. He got the joint going and sucked back on it like it was a straw feeding up a thick milkshake.

He squinted his eyes and held a lung full of smoke back as he passed me the joint. "The kids here have to relight it a bunch of times before it's done. Kind of a pain in the ass if you ask me, but what the hell."

I had never smoked this stuff before, but like Angus, I'd seen enough people doing it to have a good idea how to fake it. My lungs took in the thick smoke as a poor excuse for oxygen. It burned. I started coughing and couldn't stop.

Angus was laughing at me. I passed him back the joint as I continued to hack away. I heard the click of his lighter and saw him sucking back on it like a pro.

"As if you've never done this before," I wheezed.

He chuckled. "Guess it's like drinking scotch and then switching to rye. Same shit, different pile."

He passed me back the joint and I steeled myself for another burning experience. Wasn't as bad the second time but I started coughing anyways.

I suddenly stopped. "Angus. How can we do this? We're passing this back and forth. No offence or nothing but you're...kind of dead."

Angus laughed and reached for the joint. "I brought some of the food out of the room with me, thinking it would just drop from my hands. But nope, just like the smokes, I can hold it. I have no idea how it works but..."

He took a long, hard drag. The end of joint was glowing.

"...I'm not gonna argue with it."

He handed it back to be to me and sure enough, my fingers took hold of something real. I stared at Angus for a minute, probably long enough to be considered rude and then I poked him with my finger.

It felt like freezing water.

"Huh," Was all I could say. We continued to sit there for some time, not really minding the silence.

"So tell me, Em. What's got you down?"

"What?"

"When you came here today, you had that look like somebody had just shit in your cereal. What happened?" Cool, easy-going cowboy. He was asking, but it was hard to tell if he really cared if he got an answer or not.

I found that I didn't care. Didn't really matter what I told him. He wasn't even alive. "I was fucking this fantastic boy last Sunday and this Sunday I'm sitting in an old hospital, smoking dope with you. No offence Angus, you're great."

He didn't say anything. Part of me knew I should have been embarrassed about what I'd said, or at least curious as to what he was thinking, but I was neither. It was all good.

"Well, why the hell aren't you there fucking him tonight?"

I was staring straight ahead and seriously considering not replying at all. It seemed like a lot of work. "I just...didn't want to hold his hand."

"Now that's just odd. Not saying I'm old fashioned or nothing but anytime I made it with a girl I *had* to hold her hand. What you got against it?"

"Nothing. We work together. I just didn't want anyone talking shit."

"Fuck 'em. Do what makes you happy, Em. If you tell him you're sorry and you mean it, he'll fuck you again."

A snort of laughter jumped out of me. "Yup, that's all he's good for."

Angus started laughing too. Before I knew it we were both on the floor, howling.

"Who are you talking to?"

I stood up suddenly. In the doorway were two young boys looking at me like I'd completely lost it.

I looked at the wall and saw Angus stepping into his little white room which of course those boys had no idea even existed. He waved to me with a big stupid grin on his face. It was clear he thought it was hilarious how crazy I must have seemed at that moment.

"I...uh...here." I held out the burning joint I was pinching. "Take it."

"Whoa, seriously? Thanks!" The older looking boy said appreciatively.

"Yeah, don't mention it. No, really don't. I'd probably get thrown in jail for this. Be safe guys."

I grabbed my bag and ran out into the cool night. The sky was clear and for a few, lovely moments I stared up at the big moon. It looked like it was smiling.

I dug through my bag and found my cell. Still no missed calls. Angus was right. I had to try.

I looked through the last number to call me and dialled it. No one ever called me, so it could only be Robert.

"Hello?" He sounded tired.

"Oh shit, did I wake you?"

"Em? No, it's only...one a.m. It's okay. What's up?" he said groggily.

"Look, I just wanted to say that I'm sorry. Last week really meant a lot. I guess I just....I just got scared about what people would think. You know I've built up this wall and I just didn't know what I'd do without it."

He didn't say anything.

"Okay, I'm sorry I woke you. And I'm sorry about not holding your hand."

"Em, are you drunk?"

"What? No. Look, I just lost track of time. I had to call you. Just to let you know. Good night." I hung up.

I raced through the woods and started in a slow jog back to my house. The cool air felt good on my toasted lungs. I stopped at the 7-11 and bought a water and some gum. Anything to get rid of this taste in my mouth.

As I rounded the corner to my house, I felt my heart stop. Robert's car was in front of my building.

Somehow my legs pushed me across the street. He spotted me and got out.

"Em. I tried calling up to your place. It's the only one with your last name but whoever answered was just really angry."

"How long have you been waiting here?"

"Just a few minutes. Your phone just keeps going straight to voicemail."

"Must have died." I didn't know what to say.

"I was worried about you. You didn't sound like yourself on the phone."

I nodded. "You mean nice was unexpected?"

He laughed. Thank God. "No, you sounded sick or something."

"Oh, yeah. I was visiting someone that smokes. So gross, makes my throat hurt." I shivered a bit.

"I should let you go up." he said.

"We could sit and talk for a bit. I'd invite you up but my aunt's probably still pissed about having to answer the buzzer."

"That was your aunt?"

"Yeah. We could sit in your car?"

"Sure, yeah."

I walked around to the passenger side and slipped into the front seat. As soon as he sat down I started in.

"I don't have any friends. Like, any. I haven't had a boyfriend since college and even then it wasn't serious at all. I just...I guess I just don't know what the fuck I'm supposed to do with you. You kinda caught me by surprise."

He smiled. "I care about you a lot. I really don't care who at the lab knows."

How? How did this happen? I had done nothing to Robert except be a frosty bitch and he was here. I tried to muster some disgust at his tolerance for abuse but I couldn't. I wanted him to love me.

He put a hand to my cheek and stroked it. He leaned in closer and kissed me. My head swam, but I couldn't tell if I was still high or just happy. My hands found his face and his shoulders.

I pulled away and crawled into the back seat. I pulled him over and wrapped myself around him. I didn't care who saw us.

103

He pulled a familiar blanket around me as we did the best we could with the amount of space the backseat could afford us. I couldn't complain.

I leaned against him and looked out onto the empty night. I didn't want him to go anywhere but despite fucking him on a beach and in a car, I wasn't ready for him to come upstairs. There was something almost sacred about the last place Julia had been and I wasn't ready to give it up to another person. Not yet.

"If you hold my hand tomorrow, I promise not to pull away."

I couldn't see his face but his arms squeezed me.

"At least let me keep some of my decency by coming into work alone?"

He laughed softly and kissed my head. "Whatever you need."

I spotted him as soon as I came into the coffee shop. He was third in line and looked dishevelled but happy. My stomach dropped and then rolled over a few times as I came up beside him, but I'd already decided that I was going to do this.

After I'd left Robert's car last night, I floated up to my apartment. I was probably still high but I was also really happy. Before I fell into bed I wrote myself a note. It read *Hold his hand tomorrow.*

I looked down at my scrawling and knew that there was no way around this. I wasn't stoned anymore and the glow of last night had faded away with sleep. But I still wanted to be around him. I still wanted him.

I threw out my hand to catch his without looking and grabbed a big handful of sweater instead. I quickly walked my hand down his arm and clutched his hand. His skin was so warm.

"Jesus, Em!" he yelped.

For a split second I wanted to retreat into my former self and tell him he was an idiot or something. I wanted to crawl into a hole so no one would ever find me again. I felt like I was made of little more than glass that was about to shatter.

He turned to me and wrapped his other hand around mine. He furiously rubbed my hand with his. "Your hands are freezing!" He looked at me and smiled.

My breath caught in my throat. I tried to say something but I couldn't get it straight and then Nancy's ear piercing bark ruined any train of thought that had been forming.

"You want a latte, Em?"

I nodded too enthusiastically.

He didn't seem to care though. He smiled widely, paid for our overpriced drinks and even tipped Nancy.

"We're here early. Do you want to sit for a minute?"

I nodded again, all too eagerly. I felt like I was having an out-of-body experience. I knew I was being ridiculous but I couldn't stop myself.

We took a table by the window. I used to think it was stupid how people always wanted window seats, even when the window looked out onto highways or back alleys. But looking at the rather nondescript street that stretched out beside the cafe, I suddenly felt very grateful for a window seat. It felt like an unofficial emergency exit.

"I just about called in sick today, I'm so tired." Robert said.

"Why do you like me?"

He sat up a little straighter and looked at me oddly for a second.

"No, really. I've been a complete bitch since I came to this lab. You're not just nice to me, you actually like me. Why?" I didn't think I could handle any response he could possibly come up with.

Yes, you're right. You're a complete bitch, I'm outta here! Or maybe *I knew you were completely messed up and if I hit it at the right moment, you'd put out.* Or perhaps *I am masochistic.*

Instead he smiled and said it was because I was pretty.

I didn't go back to Creekside until that weekend. I came with a chocolate cake, paper plates and plastic forks.

Dolly was beside herself with delight. The cake was massive and yet she ate nearly half of it. No one minded though. This was a lifetime of self-deprivation coming to a chocolaty end and it was actually nice to see. I guess the fact that she couldn't gain an ounce here was part of her ease but that wasn't the point. I mean, you could learn that certain snakes were harmless and still be just as terrified of them.

Angus tried to keep up with the smiles and laughing but I could tell it was a fight. First Francine and Doug, and now Dolly. Something had changed. And me? I was alive and getting happy.

He stepped out of the white room with me and let it close up behind him before he started talking. I guess I knew this was coming. It was only a matter of time before he would get off his high horse and admit defeat.

"Look it, I know I gave you a hard time before. You know, about the whole looking up our deaths thing."

"Yeah you did. But you were right. I was more than just curious."

He nodded. "Yeah. Losing your mom and your sister would make that happen, I suppose. Trying to figure out where the hell they might have gone." He paused for second and licked his lips. He didn't want to ask but he had to. "Could you look me up?"

I nodded. "Sure thing, Angus. What's your name?"

He looked so relieved. "Thanks Em. You're a real sweetheart, you know that? Angus Joseph Brown. Last year I remember was 1986 and I'm pretty sure I was in Vancouver."

"No kidding, eh? So you've heard of Huntsville then?"

He nodded. "Yeah. Didn't want to say nothing but my own mother stayed in this joint."

I felt my eyes grow wide. "Seriously? Did you know where you were before I told you guys?"

He shook his head. "No, she was in a room upstairs and I can't make it that far. I only visited her here once and never came down this way. If it were possible, I probably would have shit myself when you told us where we were."

"Small world, eh?"

"Tiniest little clusterfuck ever."

Parents and Dinner

"I want you to come over to meet my parents."

The latte rushed up my nose and all over the table. I gasped for air as the hot, frothy drink threatened my lungs.

"Oh shit, sorry Em!" Robert was up, out of his chair and back again with a fistful of napkins before I could breathe.

"What the fuck, Robert." I finally managed. The words came out strained. Partly from a lack of air but mostly surprise.

"I just...well, I talk about you sometimes. They want to meet you."

"Robert, I can't! I can barely handle this!" I said as I wildly gestured at the space between us.

His face changed. He wasn't angry but there might have been some hurt in there.

"Look Robert, I really, really like you. More than I've ever liked anyone...like this. I just need some time." I was three inches from losing it. I couldn't lose him because I had stupidly started needing him.

He just looked at me and reached for my hand. "Okay, Em. But I'm gonna keep asking."

I felt my shoulders ease and my breathing quiet. "I hope so."

I'd gone back to Creekside twice in one week but each time was almost painful. I had no news for Angus. In 1986, the last year he remembered, there had been a few newspapers running at the time. I had dutifully checked the October obituaries, right around the World Series games, but I found nothing.

"Hey Em, I know you haven't found anything yet. I mean about me." Angus and I were standing in the dingy little hospital room after my second visit. I had brought chocolate chip cookies.

"I've been looking. Are you sure you were in Vancouver? I'm checking the obituaries for October and I can't find a thing."

He took his cap off and ran his hand over his scalp. "I dunno, Em. That's the piss poor truth of it."

"I'm going to keep looking. If I could find out about Dolly, I'm sure I can find out about you."

"Now no lying to me, alright? Don't make something up if you get tired of looking. If you do find something, no matter what, you be straight with me. Even if it turns out I went off the deep end and did something real bad, you gotta tell me." He looked desperate. It was unsettling coming from him.

"I promise. Are they getting to you?"

Angus sat down on one of the beds and sighed. "Yeah. It's like I don't know which end is up anymore. Things are getting so muddled up in my head here and I just can't even think straight. It's that glow of theirs. It's driving me crazy!"

I sat down beside him. "Okay. I'm gonna keep looking. I've gotta go now though. I've got a dinner date I can't miss."

He looked up at me. I have to admit that I was insulted at the surprised look on his face.

"Yeah, I have friends."

"I never said you didn't. But you said dinner date."

I sighed. "I'm meeting a boy's parents tonight for the first time and I would rather spend the night in jail."

"Then why the hell are you going?"

I looked down at my feet. I was wearing a pair of old sneakers. I needed to go home and change. "Because I like him."

"Well, isn't he the lucky one. Go charm those parents, Em. Tell them, especially this boy's mom, that their son is the greatest. And that you've done nothing but hold hands."

I had to laugh. I turned and started for the door.

"Thanks Angus. I'll fill you in on how it went tomorrow."

He smiled and winked at me. "I'll be waiting."

"Gees, Emily! See what a little effort can do?"

I looked into the mirror and had to admit that I looked better than usual. Julia had been helping me get ready for a date. She'd done my hair and makeup and had even picked out my clothes.

"Yeah, you're a genius. Can't wait for this to be over. After this, will you get off my back?" I said.

Julia smiled. "I know what you gave up when mom died. I just don't want to see you end up alone because you had to worry about me all this time."

"Oh please. Jude's your legal guardian, not me."

Julia snorted. "Oh yeah? Watch this." She got up and opened the door to my bedroom. "Auntie Jude! I'm on fire, help! Seriously, I lit myself on fire and I am actually burning to death!"

Nothing.

"Okay, okay. Give her a break, she's ancient."

"I don't care that she's completely incapacitated most of the time. But only because I've got you. Please try to have fun tonight?"

This was Julia to the core. Always thought of everyone else. At fourteen, she was beautiful, smart and probably one of the sweetest people I knew. I wrapped her up in my arms.

"I'd probably have more fun staying here with you." I said. "This guy's a dud, I know it."

Julia laughed. "Okay, consider him a practice run. Try out some good table manners, conversation starters, that sort of thing. Besides, I picked you out a good boob shirt. It can't be wasted on me."

I nodded. "Thanks Julia. There's cash in the cookie jar. Order some pizza or something, okay?"

I looked at myself in the mirror. I had no one to help me get ready tonight. Normally, memories of Julia left me hallow but today it calmed me. I didn't attempt anything as complicated as a boob shirt or makeup, but I did iron a shirt.

My stomach was sick before we even started dinner. I prayed that Robert's mom was against serving anything too pungent on a first meet-the-parents dinner. No fish, curries, eggs, broccoli, fried pork or beef, or liver. I think I smiled when she brought out a big dish of spaghetti.

"You never know nowadays who eats what so hopefully you're okay with pasta," his mom said as she set the dish down in front of Robert and me.

"I skipped the beef, just in case and you can add cheese if you want but you don't have to have any."

"Stop fussing and sit. I don't know why we had to skip out on the meatballs. We could've just had those on the side too." Robert's dad was pouting.

"You know I hate the smell of those rotten things. Last thing I'm gonna do is send Robert's girlfriend running from this house because it smells like a butcher shop in summer."

"My dad hunts and my mom makes meatballs out of moose meat, hence the smell." Robert explained.

"Wild game, doesn't get any better!" his dad added.

"This looks great. Thanks." I said.

Robert's mom smiled brightly at me. "Well go on now and dig in! You're our guest after all, you go first."

Now this is something I've never gotten my head around. Why are guests made to feel special by putting them on the spot? My arms couldn't move and I guess my stillness lasted just a second too long. Both his parents were staring at me.

Robert grabbed my plate and started scooping pasta on to it. "Mom, pass me down your plate. Dad, hand Em the cheese, eh?"

The three of them busied themselves with passing plates here and there, whirling the two different kinds of cheese from one side of the table to the other. I was no longer the center of attention.

It didn't last long. As soon as I had shoved the first forkful of spaghetti into my mouth, his mom started up again. Shirley? Shit, I couldn't remember.

"So Emily, Rob here tells us you pretty much keep that lab running. How long have you been doing that?"

I couldn't help it. My brain dissected her question ten different ways before I could even think of answering. Why did she want to know? What was she implying? What had Robert told her?

"Uh, well I started working in a lab about five years ago, after I'd finished my undergraduate degree. It was in Vancouver. That lab closed and I got hired on at this lab about two years ago. So, awhile I guess."

"Wow, so this must be really interesting work," she remarked.

A little laugh escaped me. "It pays my rent."

"You thinking of grad school at all?" she continued.

"I don't know. Maybe. Our boss offered me a student position the first year I was there but they pay you a lot less and you have to apply for funding. It's kind of a mess, so I just decided not to bother that year."

His dad huffed. "They sure do pay a lot less. If it wasn't for the family business, this one here wouldn't even be able to pay his rent." He pointed his fork at Robert. Joe? No, it definitely wasn't Joe. Cliff?

"Come on dad..." Robert began to protest.

"Oh don't come on dad me. It's all well and good to learn, but there comes a time when you have to take on the responsibilities of a job. Join the real world."

Robert sighed and put his fork down. It was easy to see that this wasn't the first time they had discussed this topic.

Like the rising up of gastric acid, Dumb Emily's words found my throat and burned. "No disrespect, but your son does amazing work."

"Em, it's okay," Robert said gently.

"No, it's not. I've been at the lab long enough to see that he's the only one that gets published regularly and his latest project is good enough for *Nature*. I know that may not sound like much but it's people like your son that are pushing this world forward. Medicine, economics, engineering, it's all because of research. He's just got to play this stupid grad school game awhile longer. It's just how research is set up and it sucks but your son is incredible at it. The stuff he comes up with is unlike any of the other grad students in our lab. His ideas are what keep that lab's funding from drying up."

His dad looked at me. It was a completely indecipherable look.

"Sounds like you've got a fan here, Robert." he said before shoving another forkful of pasta into his mouth.

I looked over at his mom. She was beaming.

Thanks Angus, I thought to myself. *At least I won over one of the two parents.*

"But what about the bills? Things don't pay for themselves you know!" his dad countered.

I nodded. "You're right. They don't. I just don't think Robert is coordinated enough to be anything except a researcher. Maybe he'd make money today as a plumber or an electrician but in the long run he'd be broke. Trades people make it on reputation." Oh thank you so much, Dumb Emily. Much obliged!

And then his dad did the best thing in the world. He started laughing.

"This one's got you pegged, Rob! Look out!" he howled.

No News Is Not Good News

Angus was waiting outside the white room for me. He held his hat in his hands and kept his eyes downcast. "You...didn't find nothing yet, did ya?"

My throat tightened a little at the back. "Not yet, Angus. Can you give me anything more?"

He looked down at his feet for a minute before shaking his head. "It's alright. Maybe next time."

None of them were ever hungry but they gobbled down the donuts I had brought anyways. And they were laughing. They joked about things they had read about or seen in the various magazines and papers I had brought them. They made light-hearted fun of one another.

"Oh look at the time," I said, pointing to my useless watch. The only measure of time I had was the disappearance of the food I brought. About half gone, it had been close to three hours.

Francine got up and walked me to the wall.

"You're a real sweetie, Emily." She wrapped her meaty arms around me and pulled me in. It was like hugging the friendliest marshmallow ever. "Now you take care of yourself." A few tears had gathered in the corners of her eyes.

I nodded. "Come on now, Francine. I'll be back and you'll see for yourself that I'm doing alright."

She nodded and brushed away her tears. "Yep. Go on, now. Don't need you getting raped and murdered just because we kept you past dark."

Dolly came up to me next. She was blubbering. "You be good, little Em. I'll miss you like you can't even believe!" Her

114

babyish tone had lost its annoying ring. She sounded almost angelic now.

"What's with you guys?" I asked. No one answered my question.

Doug was there with an extended hand. "Good luck, Emily."

I took it. "Buy low, sell high, right Doug?"

He laughed. "Forget that crap. Either learn the ins and outs of the market or pay someone who has. And RRSPs are always a good idea."

I looked at the three of them. "So is someone going to fill me in? Are you all heading to Disneyland or something?"

Francine shook her head. "You looking stuff up about us made us all really think about how quick it can be over and done with. With whatever stretch of life you've got left, we just want you to make the most of it."

Dolly nodded enthusiastically. "And remember that Las Vegas is *never* what it seems to be." She was being dead serious.

I fought hard against a burst of laughter and Francine's twitching mouth was no help. It was Angus's firm hand on my shoulder that kept me from insulting that adorable, but ridiculously, naive showgirl.

"Come on now, Em. It's getting late."

He came out of the room with me. As the wall curled up behind us, I looked back in and waved to the other three residents of the white room.

"So, did you draw the short straw? Your job to tell me what's going on?" I asked.

"I wish I had something to tell. They've changed, Em. It's like something is just waiting to give." He sighed and suddenly he looked very tired. "I don't know, Em. Something is changing though. All I do know is that my gut is saying maybe you shouldn't come back here."

I didn't know what to say.

"Those three, there's something changing about them. I..." he stopped himself. "I would stop wasting your precious time down here is all."

"But I still haven't found out about you yet. I'm trying, really!"

He nodded. "I know. You go on now, Em. Get back to the living, no need to be coming here so much."

I was being dismissed and I had no idea why.

Return Address

I felt empty again.

I got home just after eleven. I hadn't even thought to check my cell until then. There was a text message from Robert waiting for me.

If u have time after ure visit id like 2 C U

I don't think anything could have counteracted the hollowness inside me better than that stupid little text message.

"Hi, I just got in."

"Emily." His voice sounded rough, like he'd be sleeping.

"Oh shit, I'm so sorry, I didn't even notice what time it was. Call me whenever you get up." I slammed the phone shut.

Immediately it started to shake in my hand. It was Robert. Normally I wouldn't have picked up, but then again, normally I wouldn't have called in the first place.

"Hello?"

"Don't hang up! I was waiting up for you, but the News was so boring. I just passed out for a few minutes," he said quickly.

"I'm really sorry."

"It's alright! Besides, it's eleven on a Friday. I think it's kinda sad that I fell asleep watching the News anyway. Do you want to meet up?"

My stomach knotted. "Yeah, sure."

"Great! I'll come get you."

"No, I'll meet you. You don't need to come all the way here." I answered quickly.

The other end was quiet for a moment. "Nah, you'll take too long to get anywhere and it's dark out. I'll just come get you. I'll call you when I'm outside your place, okay?"

I thought about protesting this but what was the point? I *wanted* him to come pick me up so I wouldn't be alone for long.

"Okay, I'll see you in a bit."

The grating screech of Mr. Puggums took my attention away from the folded cell. The bony old cat sauntered over to me and sat at my feet. I picked him up and he purred loudly.

I walked into Julia's empty room and the cat rattled on. He had loved Julia. When Jude moved in after our mom had died, Mr. Puggums gave her up completely for Julia. Who could blame him? Julia was perfect.

My hand started shaking. It took me a second to realize that it was my phone.

"Hey, I'm downstairs. Are you ready to come down?"

"Uh, where did you want to go?"

"Maybe we could drive into Vancouver. Get a late dinner or something?"

I looked around Julia's empty room and suddenly felt like I shouldn't leave.

"Come up for a second. You can park anywhere on the street, no one really cares."

"Alright," he sounded surprised. I had not once invited him up. "Three-eleven?"

"Yeah, that's right."

I buzzed him up a couple of minutes later with Mr. Puggums still roaring away in my arms. The cat let out a ragged greeting as Robert came in.

He smiled and scratched the cat's head. "I didn't know you had a cat. Or that you smoked."

"Oh. Sorry about that. I don't, it's my aunt. Guess I just don't notice it anymore. Normally she keeps the window open so it's not that bad."

"It's pretty windy out, I can see why she'd close it."

But it wasn't that at all. The cold night air was coming in from somewhere. I put Mr. Puggums down, much to his disappointment, and ran into the living room.

A cluster of cigarettes were smouldering away in the ashtray beside my aunt's chair. All the butts were burning up now. The television was still on and the living room window was wide open, kicking up curls of cigarette smoke with unseen wind currents.

But there was no snoring.

My hand went to her throat without thinking. I couldn't find a pulse and her skin was cold.

"Oh my God." I whispered.

"Em, is she dead?"

I didn't know what to say. He stepped in front of me and checked her pulse for himself.

Just then, she sat up straight and screamed.

"Who the hell are you? What are you doing in my house?" She pushed her rickety body up and Robert jumped about three feet in the air.

"Holy shit, she's alive!" he exclaimed.

My heart was pounding and I swear had I drank anything that day, I would have peed my pants. And then I started laughing. It was insane, off the deep end laughing.

Robert started in too until we were both on the floor in tears. Mr. Puggums was nosing around both of us, trying to figure out what was going on.

"Emily? Who is this pervert?" Jude demanded.

That made me burst into another fit of nervous laughter. Between gasps of air, I finally managed to ease her mind a little. "He's...he's my pervert, Jude."

This made Robert lose it all over again.

It was one in the morning by the time Jude was able to fall asleep again. Robert and I were down the hall in my room when her snoring started up.

"Did she have duel exhausts installed or that all stock?" he asked, smiling.

"I don't even notice it anymore."

"How long have you two lived together?"

"Since my mom died. I was about nineteen, I guess."

"Why?"

"Why not?"

He chuckled. "I mean, it's not like you were a minor or anything."

"Maybe I just really like her company."

He snorted. "I admit, that didn't cross my mind."

I was laying across his chest in my tiny bed. I breathed him in and realized that it was time I started spreading out this crazy. I didn't need it to eat away at me anymore.

"My sister was a minor. It was just easier having my aunt move in than deal with all the Family Services bullshit."

"Your sister? You have a sister?"

"Had. She died." I felt small and scared but his arm around me wasn't moving.

He didn't say anything for a long time. "Em? How'd she die?"

I sighed. It wasn't that I didn't want to tell him. If anything, it was a sigh of relief.

"She killed herself when she was fifteen." I rolled out from under his arm and reached into the drawer of my nightstand. I took out the only picture I knew of where Julia looked beautiful and I looked happy.

"This was her. She was about fourteen here."

Robert gently took the picture, holding it by the edges. His care of it was sweet.

"You both look really happy. And you look short."

I laughed. "Yeah, I know. She was beautiful. And tall."

He waited a moment before asking. "Em? Do you know why she did it?"

I was back on his chest as I nodded. "Yeah. She was fucking one of her teachers. I found out about it and threatened to call the cops. He got all scared and broke it off. Bastard had a wife and kid. Got my sister knocked up and then just threw her aside like she was nothing."

After all this time my anger was just as raw and ready.

"I'm sorry, Em. I know you must really miss her." His arm tightened around me. It helped.

I smushed my fist across my eyes to blot out the quickly forming tears. "Just wish I had done something."

"Oh Em." He wrapped his other arm around me and held me so close it was almost hard to breathe. "It wasn't your fault. She loved you and wouldn't want you to think that."

"How do you know that?" I had tried to come out sounding accusatory, but instead my voice was small and pleading. I wanted to believe what he had said and needed to know how he could have made that kind of deduction.

"Because I know you."

I sniffed and turned my face into his chest. I was soaking his t-shirt with tears but that didn't matter. As long as he was making me feel better I decided to throw another innermost secret out there.

"I burned his house down."

"What? Whose house?"

"The teacher that was fucking my sister. He and his family were away when I burned his house down."

Suddenly Robert's body began shaking. I sat up, worried that he was having a seizure after having been exposed to an excessive amount of my insanity. No, he was laughing.

"Why are you laughing? This is serious. I'm a horrible person! They lost everything!"

Robert sat up and sucked in air as he tried to calm himself. "No, Em. You did. They just had to stay in a hotel for a few months and get the family pictures redone."

It wasn't until three in the morning that the heaviness of sleep started to interrupt our thoughts and make us misuse words.

"Maybe I should go," Robert said as he stood up to leave.

"You can crash here if you want. It's kinda late to be driving." I was barely able to stand.

He smiled. "I forgot my toothbrush."

"Oh hell, get out of here!" I said as I dramatically waved him away. "Nah, I'm just shitting you. I've always got extras around. And I mean like new extras, not the old ones that you keep to scrub tiles and crap like that."

I wandered out ahead of him to the bathroom, thinking he was right behind me. When I got to the bathroom, I realized I was alone. I made the short trip back to my bedroom to see Robert holding a pink envelope.

"Robert?"

"Whose this from?" he asked.

"My dad." Robert's face was twisted up as he continued to stare at the pink envelope. "Do you recognize the name or something?"

He shook his head. "Have you ever been to this place?" he asked, pointing to the return address written tightly in the envelope's upper right-hand corner.

"Nope. I get one every year for my birthday. Same place." Suddenly I felt a very unexpected wave of guilt push away my sleepiness. "I've never even met him."

Robert looked at me for a second too long and then he smiled. "Come on. I need to brush my teeth and fall asleep."

I didn't think I'd be able to fall asleep. Robert's unease about my dad's card was obvious. Was it because I had never once visited him? It was honestly one part of my life that I didn't think he'd care about. After everything I had told him, a silly birthday card from a completely absent father had made him stop and think about what he had just gotten into. It was hard to fight off these thoughts as they wormed into my mind.

I wondered if Robert could tell how unsettled I was. Every time I was about to jump out of bed and hide in Julia's room, his arms got a little tighter around me.

I stared at him across the shiny diner table. Orange juice and coffee had been dropped off for us and the smell of frying bacon and flapjacks was almost enough to make me forget that strange look he had on his face the night before. But not quite.

"You seemed so messed up when you saw that envelope on my desk last night. Why?"

He choked on his juice. I didn't move a muscle to help him clean any of it up.

He mopped up the mess with a handful of napkins and looked up at me a few times. After setting aside the wet, sticky mound of paper, he started working on his own hands with another one. I didn't say a word. *Let it eat at him,* I thought.

"My mom used to work there," he finally said.

"Where?"

"At the hospital. I guess I was just surprised when I saw the address, that's all."

"What hospital?"

He looked at me. "The return address, it's a psychiatric hospital."

"What?"

Robert just nodded. "Em, why have you never written him back?" There was no accusation in his tone, but it broke my heart all the same.

"My mom told me not to. That he wouldn't have wanted it." I sounded small and pathetic. It was the truth but sometimes that's a poor excuse for the things we do or, in this case, don't do.

"Why would he have put his return address on there?"

I shrugged. "I asked my mom that once and she said that it gave him peace of mind to know that if it got lost in the mail or if there wasn't enough postage that he would get it back and could send it out right the second time."

A busty waitress settled our plates in front of us and slipped out as if she could smell the tension and wanted no part of it.

"Well...things are a little different now. Would you want to go see him?"

I stared down at my eggs. I had ordered them sunny side up but I was seriously regretting that choice at the moment. They looked disgusting.

"Hey, Emily. I'm sorry. Look, don't worry about it, okay? We don't have to talk about it right now."

I wanted to cry. I had been inches from a meltdown and he had backed off, just the way I needed him to. Every fragile seam that had held me together was torn and he was so gentle with me, as if he didn't want the stuffing to fall out.

"Come on, eat your eggs before they get cold. Nothing worse than cold eggs. They taste like ass."

Thankfully, they were still warm.

Hi Stanley,

It's Emily and I am currently 26 years old. Thanks for the birthday cards you've been sending all these years. I thought I'd finally write you after all this time to let you know a little bit about the person you seem to think is worth remembering year after year. I work in a lab. Basically I help out the students with their projects, order stuff, keep things running. I'm thinking about going to graduate school soon too.

Mom died in 2004 in a car accident. I had a little sister named Julia but she passed away too in 2008. I live with mom's sister Jude and her cat, Mr. Puggums.

If you're ever up to getting together for a meal or something, I'd be happy to come down to Appletown. It's okay if you'd rather not though. I'm not really sure what else to say except thanks. The birthday cards are really special to me.

Emily

I read the letter over and over again. I finally settled on writing out a second copy with nicer penmanship. I also changed *Stanley* to *Dad* and squeezed in a *Love* before signing my name.

I got a letter back three days later. I had no idea the postal services of Canada could be so efficient, or that Stanley would have had anything to say so quickly.

"Em? What's wrong?"

"Huh?"

Robert smiled at me from across the table. "I've been talking for the last twenty minutes. I started saying things like blue toaster, gopher phones, red banana."

"What? Why would you talk about that kind of stuff?"

He chuckled. "To see if you were listening."

I shook my head. "Look, I'm sorry. I just..."

He waited.

"Stanley wants to meet me."

"Stanley?"

"My dad. I took your advice and wrote him. He got back to me like three days later, says he wants to meet me."

Robert sat up straighter. "Wow, that's great!"

I nodded. "Yeah. I guess."

"What? You don't want to anymore?"

"No, it's not that. I just...I've never met him before. What I am supposed to say?"

"I don't know. But you should go."

"Why?"

"Why'd you write him?"

"Because you made me feel like shit."

He laughed. "I don't think the jury would buy it."

I sighed. "I just...what if he hates me? Or I hate him? Or we just have nothing to say to one another?"

Robert shrugged. "Yeah, I guess that could happen. I doubt it though. You wrote him because you wanted to and he wrote back because he wants to meet you."

I chewed on my lower lip. "I don't know."

"I'll go with you."

"Really?"

He nodded. "Yeah, for sure. Let's book our time off tomorrow."

Appletown

The hospital was a squat grey building. The windows were like small, suspicious eyes. There was no big announcement, no neon sign about who lived there and why. There was a completely unnoticeable sign that read *Appletown Psychiatric Hospital.* That was it.

I felt stuck to my chair. I couldn't move. I don't know how long Robert had been calling my name before he resorted to shaking me.

"Oh gees!" I jumped up and hit my head on the roof of Robert's car.

"Em! Sorry! Are you okay?" Robert asked.

My hand instinctively went to my wounded noggin. "Yeah, sure. Sorry, I'm just..."

"It's okay. You told your dad one o'clock, right?"

I nodded. He pointed to the dashboard clock. The glowing green numbers read 1:04.

"Okay." I exhaled and reached for the car door. "I don't know how long I'll be."

Robert took my hand and squeezed it. "I have some papers I have to read before the conference in L.A. next week. I've got lots to keep me busy."

"You're not going to wait here, are you?"

"Sure, why not?"

I started shaking my head. "No, Robert. Go back to the motel or get some food or something."

"Well, that motel smells weird. I'll wait for you here."

I was going to argue but he was right. The motel did smell weird. And the truth was that I wanted him here. Just in case.

"Okay. I'll see you in a bit."

My legs were unsteady as I walked up to the hospital's front doors. A stern looking nurse eyed me up and down. "Can I help you?" Yes, it really sounded like that's what she wanted to do.

"Now, Peggy! Keep that sass to yourself. This here is Emily!"

I turned around. Coming up behind me was a man, probably in his fifties, with a head of thick, dark hair that was greying at his temples. He was slight but not thin. He wore a grey button down shirt and had the sleeves rolled up and the tails tucked into a pair of blue jeans.

"Stanley?" My voice was pathetically small.

He smiled and shook his head. "No. I work with Stanley though and he told me you were coming. Not too many new faces come around here, so it was easy to guess that the only twenty-something I've seen around here must be Stanley's long awaited guest."

"So, you're his doctor?"

He nodded and stepped closer with an outstretched hand. I took it. "Dr. Mackeil. It is very nice to meet you. Stanley is just getting up and asked me to come meet you if you showed before he was ready."

"Get up? It's one o'clock in the afternoon."

Dr. Mackeil just smiled. "Your father is undergoing something called electroconvulsive therapy. Basically, we use electricity to induce a seizure in his brain. We're not sure exactly how but these mini seizures can have a big impact on certain psychiatric conditions. Mainly it's used for depression, but there has been some research to suggest that it may work for persons suffering from schizophrenia as well."

My palms began to sweat and my stomach twisted. I couldn't look at him. We walked towards the hospital cafeteria.

"I'm sorry. He told me that you knew he had schizophrenia."

I looked up suddenly and started nodding like an idiot. "Yeah, he mentioned it in his letter. I just didn't..."

Dr. Mackeil just looked at me and smiled.

"Nothing. Is he taking any medications?" I didn't actually care, nor would I understand what the names of the medications meant, but I felt like I had to say something.

"Yes but we've had to administer these medications fewer and fewer times since he began treatment three weeks ago." He smiled again, that non-descript, let's all just take a breather smile. Suddenly he turned to his left and waved.

I turned around and saw a man shuffling into the cafeteria. He was in brown pyjamas and he looked a bit worn. His dark hair, dark like mine, was pointing in all different directions. His big, brown eyes sagged and his olive skin looked weathered. Had he not looked so tired, it would have been easy to describe this man as handsome.

"Stanley. Emily and I have just been having a little chat. How about you two take a table by the window?" Dr. Mackeil suggested.

Stanley looked around the room anxiously. "Sure, sounds good doc."

He didn't look at me as he made his way over to the window. The doctor smiled again and left.

"I saw you in your car," he said as we each took our seats. "I thought maybe you were going to run."

I laughed a little. "Thought about it."

"Because I'm crazy?" he said quickly. It was more of an accusation than a question.

I felt my stomach knot up and my heart start to thump. My throat threatened to close up that very minute but somehow I managed a pathetic *No*.

He seemed to calm down a little. "Sorry. I don't get any visitors."

I nodded. "I...uh. It's just that we've never met. That's why I was scared about coming in. Not because this is a mental hospital."

It was bizarre watching him dissect each one of my words. There was no trust but he was trying.

"So, you said you work in a lab. What sorts of things do you do there?"

"Well, mainly cancer research. I'm an assistant, so I order lab supplies and help with the experiments."

"You're a helper?" He might as well have just said *That's it? That's all you amounted to?*

I swallowed hard before I answered him. My throat felt like it had been stuffed with paper towels. "Yeah, I guess so."

"Who's that out in the car?"

For a second I had no idea what he was talking about. I turned and looked out the window and saw Robert sitting in his car.

"Oh, that's Robert. He's a researcher at the lab."

"He's your boss?"

"No, not at all."

"But you do the leg work for him, right?"

My head was trying to stay two steps ahead of this man's train of thought but I couldn't. It was too sporadic, too mistrustful.

"I help him."

"So he's like your boss?"

"No."

"But he tells you what he needs done, is that right?"

"Yeah."

Stanley, my father, suddenly sat up straighter. "So you're messing around with your boss."

I felt like I had just been punched in the gut. "No. It's not like that."

"That's just what your mother was like too. She messed around with her boss and got knocked up with your little sister. I'm still not sure about you. I want a DNA test."

Now that was a knee to my stomach. "Why are you doing this?"

I was about to break. The old Emily could have handled this. The old Emily wouldn't have even bothered in the first place to meet this man.

"You'd better go," he said. He stood up and staggered out of the cafeteria.

I felt like my hurt was a living thing and it was eating me from the inside out. I started crying and then I was sobbing. I don't think I was there for long before I felt a hand on my shoulder. I turned around suddenly.

It was Dr. Mackeil. "Emily? I'm sorry that didn't go as well as we'd hoped. He really was looking forward to seeing you."

I wiped my face dry with my sleeve and stood up. "Some progress you've made."

I burst out the front doors of the hospital. The sunshine was blinding and I felt like I was going to fall over. My balance came back and I took a few deep breaths. But there was nothing.

My rage had come back. And there was only one person that deserved it.

I pulled open the passenger side door and grabbed my bag from the front seat. Robert, who had been sleeping while my father called me and my mother sluts, sat up suddenly.

"Em?" he said sleepily. "Em? How'd it go?"

I slid my bag over my shoulder and slammed the car door shut. I had seen a Greyhound bus depot on our way to the hospital. It wouldn't take me long to get there.

"Em!" Robert shouted. I could hear him running up behind me. Part of me willed him to stay away but most of me wanted him to come closer so I could tear him to pieces.

He jumped in front of me and put his hands on my shoulders. "Em? What happened?"

I shrugged him off and kept walking. "I'm taking a bus home. Go on your own or stay in this shit hole for a night, I really don't care."

He caught up with me and this time held me still. "Em! Don't do this! Don't run away from me. What happened?"

I couldn't hold it back. "This is all your fault! Why couldn't you just mind your own business? Why'd you have to push me to do this? To write him?"

"Em, I..."

"Don't call me that! Go run back to mommy and daddy for another month's rent and leave me the fuck alone!"

He took a step back. That bite had drawn blood.

"What?"

"You heard me. Instead of sitting here, pointing out all the ways I'm a coward, why don't you grow a pair and figure your own shit out. I don't need him and I don't need you!"

This time I ran away. The tears started coming again because I knew that this time, he wasn't going to come after me.

I had booked a week off work to meet Stanley. I spent the rest of the week in my crappy apartment. There was no one to visit, no one to call. There was nothing again.

The Friday was particularly beautiful. The only reason I went out was because it was too hot to stay in.

I had no route in mind but somehow I ended up at the forest. My forest. My feet started going down the chewed out path to find the old hospital.

They'd want to know why I hadn't come by in so long. Well, let's see. I met my father for the first time and he basically told me that I was whore and my mother had been one too.

And then I dismissed Robert.

I had nothing to bring them this time. Hopefully they wouldn't notice. Dolly would still be beside herself with glee that she had made it to a real casino and then died the very same day. Francine would say sarcastic snips that became less cruel and more endearing each day. Doug might be upset. I didn't have a paper for him.

And Angus. He was the odd man out now and I couldn't help but feel completely and utterly responsible for his loneliness. I was not prepared for what was actually waiting for me in the old hospital.

Lonely Ghost

I sat on the rusted bed closest to the magically disappearing wall and waited. I had nothing to do but wait. The day was so lovely that it almost made the hospital look nice. The only thing, however, that could truly save it was a book of matches and some gasoline but I hadn't even remembered to bring cookies.

After more than an hour of waiting, the wall started to peel away. Angus stepped out and sighed. He didn't know I was there.

"Hey cowboy."

He jumped. "Jesus!"

I stood up and held by hands out in mock surrender. "Easy! It's just me!"

His hand had gone to his heart and he was breathing heavy.

"It doesn't work anymore, remember?" I said, nodding to his chest.

He nodded. "I just didn't think you'd come back. Thought I was alone now."

"What are you talking about?"

"They're gone, Em. All three of them. I've been alone since you left."

My stomach twisted into an uncomfortable knot. "What? Where?"

He smiled but it was a tired smile. Like he'd given up. "They just kind of changed once you told them how they died. I don't see what the point of it all was but it did something to them."

I nodded as I pictured Francine and Doug after I'd told them about their deaths. They had become angelic. "I would've come back sooner. I'm sorry, Angus, I didn't know."

He shrugged. "I dunno, maybe that was the key. Maybe that's what I need to get out of this hell hole. Each minute is stretching out to hours and then days, and I'm all alone. And...well, you know."

"No, I don't. What were you gonna say?"

Angus sat down on the closest rusted bed and it squealed in protest beneath him. "I feel old. I've never felt like that, ever. It's just not right the way I'm feeling."

Something was nagging at me. Something about this wasn't right. Sure, I felt like crap because he felt so badly but there was something else.

Just then a noise made us both turn to the room's doorway. Two boys were standing there.

"Sorry. We didn't think anyone was here."

They wheeled around and started down the hall but I could just hear them.

Lucky gramps! I'd come here with her anytime!

My heart started pounding. I turned to look at Angus but I don't think he'd heard them.

I reached out and that human instinct to reach out in return overtook Angus. The skin of his hand was rough and cool and his bones were like knobbed twigs.

I met his eyes and they were just as wide as I think mine must have been.

"What the fuck?" was all that came out. I'm not sure who said it.

In the Flesh

Angus stood up from the bed and it squealed at his departure.

"You shouldn't weigh anything. Why do you weigh anything?"

He took a few steps towards the doorway, paused and then continued on. I picked up my bag and followed.

He steeled himself as he reached for the front door of the hospital. He pulled on it and it swung open just as it would for anyone.

"Holy fucker," he whispered to himself. There was reverence in his statement.

He stepped out into the day and shielded his eyes from the bright sunlight. It was early afternoon now and warm. He took a deep breath of air and exhaled it dramatically.

"What's going on, Angus?"

"I don't have a fucking clue but it's better than in there," he said, nodding to the hospital.

"How long have they been gone?"

"What? Oh, I dunno. Maybe five days."

"Are you hungry? Thirsty?"

Angus paused for a second and looked at me like I'd just said the most amazing thing. "I'm starving! My mouth feels like it's full of sand!"

"Jesus, you haven't eaten or drank anything in five days, no wonder you feel ancient!" I reached into my bag and pulled out a half drunk bottle of water. It felt warm but I didn't think he'd be too choosy.

"Well now, I had some stuff in the room that you'd brought us the last time. We had a bit of a store going that I guess I've been a little more interested in as of late." He sat down on the hospital steps and drank the rest of the water in one long gulp. "But I haven't felt like this till just now. I don't think my parts are working yet cause I haven't had to make once."

"What?"

"You know, go to the bathroom. Haven't had the need. Maybe it was you showing up and getting me outta that room."

My head was running with a million thoughts, but it finally began to settle on the here and now. "Okay, let's get you home."

Jude wasn't home yet. I thought for a brief instant of letting Angus have Julia's room, but the feeling of just having been punched in the gut nixed that idea pretty quickly. I wasn't ready for that at all.

"Okay, you'll stay in my room and I'll stay in the spare."

He looked at me for a second, but leave it to the cowboy to know when to just say thanks.

"Thank you, Em."

I nodded. "Come on, the kitchen is this way. Not much there, but whatever you can scrounge up is for the taking. If you see a pack of Marlborough laying around, please refrain. They belong to Jude and she'll shit herself if you take them. Let me know if you need more, I'll get them."

"Your aunt gonna mind me being here?"

"Yeah, probably, but not too much we can do about it. This is pretty much my place. I pay the rent on it so I think she'll get over it pretty quickly."

"Maybe I could pitch in. You know, cook or something."

I started laughing. "Wait till you meet my aunt. You'll see why that probably won't go over so well."

He looked around the kitchen, marvelling at its ugliness and tangibility.

"Angus, what is this?" I asked.

"I have no idea, Em."

I nodded. "Well, until we figure it out, try to take it easy. Enjoy yourself I guess, who knows how long you're gonna be here for."

He sat down at the rarely used kitchen table and sighed. "This is something else. I've been dead for how long? And here I am, sitting in your kitchen. Mind if I make some coffee?" he asked, nodding towards the coffee maker curled up on the kitchen counter.

"By all means, help yourself. There's probably creamer in the fridge and the sugar is in that cupboard with the cups."

He found everything effortlessly and got straight to it. I left him and went to the bathroom. I caught myself in the mirror for a second and decided to keep on moving. No point in stopping to ask questions. There were no answers there.

I found the bottle I was looking for and headed back to the kitchen.

"Hey, cowboy. Take these. I have no idea how malnourished you are but I'm guessing with all the crap I was bringing you guys that you're not in the best of shape."

He looked at the bottle of multivitamins. "But these are for women!"

I started laughing. "It's not like you're going to grow tits or anything. Just take them!"

I sat down at the kitchen table and saw that two cups had been laid out alongside the sugar bowl and carton of cream. He carried over the coffee pot, filled each cup, set his vitamins down and returned the pot to its nest. As he settled down across from me he popped open the bottle of vitamins and took one.

"I know better than to argue with a brunette," he said as he took a swig of his coffee.

I couldn't help but smile. "Was your mama a brunette?"

He smiled and began mixing sugar and cream to make a descent cup of coffee. "As a matter of fact, she was. And anytime I didn't do something she said I should, I was sorry for it. If I'd listened to her, my life would've rolled out differently."

I smiled and brought the cup of black coffee to my nose. I breathed it in and felt the memories of early mornings with my mom in this very seat, drinking her black coffee. "Yeah, moms really do know best."

I hadn't expected it, but Angus charmed his way into Jude's bedroom by the time I had to head back to work. She distrusted him for about two seconds. I thought about going back to my own room but decided against it. Julia was almost palpable in her room and I didn't want to be alone.

Nothing had come to mind as to why Angus was whole now. I hadn't set foot in a church since the day they baptized Julia so I had no faith to go on. All I knew was that he looked good and I'd seen my aunt eat dinner for the first time in recent memory. This was working out well for pretty much everyone so far.

Lonesome Emily

The lab's fluorescent lights were harsh. One week off had been enough to make me notice all the infuriating things about the lab. Noxious smells, blinding lights, stupid grad students and an even dumber boss. My stomach tightened as I walked past Robert's office, but the door was closed. I felt myself relax. He wasn't in yet. He never closed the door to his office when he was in.

And I would have continued to appreciate that closed door except for the fact that he never came in that day. I thought about asking someone where he was but I just couldn't. It would have been analogous to admitting that I missed him.

That night I came home to find Jude's recliner empty and the television moved. Snuggled up together on the ratty old green couch were my aunt, looking surprisingly lovely, and Angus. A huge bowl of popcorn sat on their blanketed lap and they were smiling together at something on the television. Angus looked up and smiled.

"Well hello there. How'd it go at the lab?"

"Yeah, it was fine. How are you guys?"

Jude beamed. "Oh good, good. When we were out getting popcorn I saw some of those little jujubes that you used to like so much when you were little and got you a pack. They're on the counter. Why don't you grab them and come have a sit?"

I turned around and there on the counter was a bright green and pink plastic package, heralding the sweet bits of nostalgia within.

"Thanks, Jude. Uh, how much do I owe you?"

"Oh heavens no. I haven't been to Bingo in a week, still have some money kicking around. You go on and take them, they're for you."

I almost started crying. "Thanks. I'm super tired so I'm gonna take a nap for a bit. I'll see you two later."

They both waved, the cowboy and the anorexic.

The next day at the lab was the same. The door to Robert's office stayed closed.

"George!"

He stopped short and his shoulders visibly tensed. It was clear he wanted to run.

"Oh, hey Emily. How was your week off?"

"Where' Robert? Is he sick?" I demanded.

George's face looked like it had a big question mark drawn on it. "Robert? He's gone. I guess you missed his goodbye email."

Email? There hadn't been anything from him in my inbox. I nodded and turned away from George. I heard him scuttle away as I sat back down at my desk.

I searched through my work email but there was nothing from him about leaving. I closed my account and then opened George's. I had pretty much everyone's passwords. I rarely used them, but today was an exception. Robert was gone and I had no idea where.

Lab mates,

After much consideration I have accepted a position at Dunnell's lab in Toronto. I have learned so much from each and every one of you and will miss you all. Thank you for the support and encouragement these past four years and best of luck with your work.

Sincerely,
Robert

I sucked in a deep breath but it couldn't keep this feeling away. My head was spinning and my gut felt like it was holding in a violent ocean. I stood up and stumbled towards the bathroom, but there was no way I was making it down that long hallway. I settled on the nearest garbage can and began vomiting, right in the middle of the fucking lab.

"Emily? Emily? Are you okay?"

It was Lynn. "Yeah, I'm fine." No, I wasn't. I coughed a few times and tried my best to spit out what was left in my mouth, but that's a taste that doesn't give up easily. When I finally stood up, Lynn was there with a cup of water.

"Thanks. " I grumbled. The water felt amazing against my burned throat. I threw the paper cup in the garbage and began bundling it up.

Without a word, Lynn took the black plastic bag from me and finished tying it up herself.

"Go home, Emily. I'll let the boss know you weren't feeling well."

I nodded, gathered my stuff and left. As I passed through the doors to the lab, I wondered if I could ever go back, knowing that Robert would never be there again.

I stayed in bed for the rest of the week. Both Jude and Angus brought me water and soup, most of which ended up being thrown out. It wasn't that I was overwhelmed with grief and pain. I just didn't give a fuck. There was nothing left for me. My baby sister was still dead, my father hated me and Robert was gone. I had nothing again.

I didn't go back to work until the following Monday. A blond woman from admin was there, talking Lynn's head off enthusiastically. I couldn't remember her name but she looked like a Nancy.

"So we need to make people aware! You can see why donating is so important."

Lynn smiled uncomfortably. "Yeah, it's not that I don't want to. It's just that they don't pay much here and I'm pretty broke..."

"One less meal out, skip a few coffees and ta-da! You've got your donation!"

I knew what Lynn made and there were already no dinners out. Maybe the occasional coffee, but I doubted that. She was broke all the time. But she was painfully sweet.

"Well, I get paid tomorrow. Maybe I'll see what I have left over after rent..."

That was it.

"Hey, Nancy!"

The blond woman spun around. "Excuse me?"

"What's going on here?"

Sensing another change-purse to shake, this Nancy-woman smiled and started in on her spiel.

"I'm going to fly to Maui in two months and hike Mount Haleakala to raise awareness for breast cancer."

"Oh, so you're taking Lynn with you?"

The Nancy-woman's smile faded and she looked utterly confused. "No, I'm going. I'm asking Lynn if she would like to make a donation to my campaign."

"Oh I see. You're raising money for breast cancer research."

The smile was back. "Yes! Exactly! And that's just what I was saying to Lynn here, that it is so important that we continue to raise money and awareness for this important cause."

"And you're buying your plane ticket there?"

"Well, no, but that's because I'm doing the fundraising and training."

"So it's like a reward?"

She smiled again. "Well, I guess so. No reason we can't have some fun while doing these great things for mankind! Or should I say, womankind!" She laughed at her own, stupid joke.

I nodded. "Yeah, you're probably right. I just don't get why you have to go to Maui to do it. Don't you think the money for your trip would be better spent on supplies for labs like the ones here? And as for the reward, are you aware that you're hassling someone who regularly puts in eighty hour work weeks, trying to find treatments for people with all kinds of cancer?"

"Well, uh, it's also about raising awareness."

"I wouldn't give you two cents to go on this joke of a fundraiser trip. Pass out the collection plate at your next Tupperware party and leave the below-poverty-line grad student alone, alright?"

I turned away and heard Lynn's light footsteps quickly come up behind me. "Thanks Emily."

I nodded. "Now get back to work. We're not paying you five cents an hour to sit around."

She giggled and hopped over to her desk. Being kind was exhausting, but throwing some lashing out into the mix made it easier to swallow.

The apartment sounded empty when I got home. I nearly pissed myself when I heard hacking coming from the bathroom. The door was open and Angus was there, leaning over the sink. He turned and looked at me as he wiped a trail of bright red blood off his chin.

"Jesus, Angus! What happened?"

His smile was tired and it was like he suddenly came into view. His cheeks had a sunken in look as if he never ate and his eyes were blood shot.

"Are you hungover?"

He shook his head and laughed a little. "No. I could be wrong but I think I'm dying. This feels awfully familiar."

My gut felt like it had just dropped three feet. "What?"

"Look it, don't tell your aunt, alright? I just... I can't see why I'd get the second chance at this life, I must be dying."

"Come on. Let's get you to the hospital."

He turned back to the sink and started rinsing the blood away. He took a few gulps of water. "I've got no I.D., no insurance. They won't take me."

"I'll say I found you. They have to treat you. It's like a fuck-aren't-we-nice-law or something."

The cowboy looked tired but he still chuckled. "Em, I don't know why I'm here right now, but so long as I am, how's about we make the most of it. If you haven't already noticed, I'm sweet on your aunt. Just let me have this little bit of time."

I would have said yes. The thought of my aunt being happy for once in her life made me surprisingly happy. And just because I had condemned myself to being alone didn't mean anyone else had to be miserable. I wasn't so heartless as to deny these basic truths and like I said, I would have said yes. But the phone rang.

Jude

Nobody likes hospitals. Even people that work in hospitals don't like hospitals. They smell bad. Between the vomit, diarrhea and disinfectant, hospitals smell like the dead cleaning out their coffins.

Today was no exception. My aunt was on oxygen and sleeping peacefully. The doctor gave me a mix of words like chronic obstructed pulmonary disorder, smoking, hypoxia, dying. Jude's lungs weren't working anymore.

Angus and I waited there for hours in silence. Finally, she woke up.

Angus took her hand and kissed her on her forehead. She tugged her lifesaving mask away and pulled Angus close to her and kissed him. I was about to leave the room when she held her hand out to me.

"Angus. Give us a minute."

He squeezed her hand and went out into the hallway.

"Hey, Jude. Well this sucks." I swallowed hard and caught a sob that had been waiting just inside my throat.

She smiled. "Sure does. Look it, when your mom died, there was insurance money. I was going to save it for Julia to go to school but... well, anyway. Go grab my purse."

I brought the rhinestone covered sac over to her.

"Keychain." It was clear that words were getting harder and harder for her as each breath became more and more precious.

I pulled out her ring of keys quickly and held it up to her. She weakly pointed to a small, silver key.

"Westpoint Bank, Box 1983. It's all there. Have some fun, sweetie."

I smudged away a few rogue tears.

"Maybe you and that nice boy can go on a vacation."

A surprised laugh escaped me but I nodded anyway. "Yeah, that sounds like a plan."

"Okay."

"Uh, I'll go get Angus."

She looked grateful. I wasn't hurt that she wanted to spend whatever time she had left with the cowboy and not her distant niece. I know that had I been the one in the bed, I would only want one other person there, and it wouldn't have been her.

Jude died three days later. I got a call just as I was leaving the hospital. It was my dick of a boss, trying to chew me out for taking the extra time off.

"Fuck you, I quit."

And that was that. I had so few expenses over the years that I had actually been able to save some money. I'd be okay to mope around my crummy apartment for a little while.

Angus stayed at the hospital. I was on a bus home when something I passed caught my eye. A bank. An old bank.

Westpoint.

I pulled the line to stop the bus and luckily the next drop off wasn't too far away. It only took me five minutes to make it back to the bank.

A small woman in a tight black suit that smelled of no-nonsense except on Fridays greeted me coldly at the door. I was clearly not the kind of clientele she was used to.

"Yeah, hi. I have a security box here."

"Do you have your key?"

I nodded and held up the small silver key Jude had given me. It was better than a passport.

"Follow me." She led me past the counters and into a back room, through a locked door and then another one.

"Box number?"

"1983." I answered quickly.

We passed through another door and then into a room lined with silver drawers, each with their own special number and their own secrets.

She took me to the furthest wall and effortlessly slid a key I didn't even realize she had been holding into the silver box marked 1983.

"Your key, miss."

Awkwardly, I pushed my key into a keyhole that neighboured the one currently occupied. We turned at the same time and the drawer opened effortlessly. She didn't make a move to touch the drawer's contents.

"Miss, if you'd like to view the contents now we have private rooms for our clients."

I pulled on the small handle of the metal box that perfectly filled the drawer called 1983.

This compact, serious woman closed the drawer, returned my key to me and led me out of the room and into a small, gently lit side room. It had one chair and a small table with a phone.

"Please, take as much time as you need. Call when you are ready to return the box to the vault."

She closed the door before I could say thanks or fuck you.

The box opened easily and inside was a bankbook and a note. The book had *Westpoint* stenciled across its leather cover in gold, serious letters.

I set the book down and picked up the neatly folded note. It was in Jude's elegant and almost pretentious scrawl.

Hey Kiddo,

Either I'm dead or just about. If I didn't tell you about this then Mr. Wilson would have been the one to tell you about this. But either way, you've got it now. This is the money from your mother's accident. They paid out pretty good. A hundred thousand dollars. Had to pay a lawyer quite the fee, nearly ten thousand and then some money went to your mom's burial. I've had to borrow a little smidge here and there but there's plenty left over for you to take care of yourself and send Julia off to school. Knowing you, you'd hand the whole lot over to her but I

*hope you don't. Your mom loved you too and would have
wanted to see you both get something out of this mess.*

I love you,
Jude

She'd written this before Julia had died. I was crying again.
The ink on the page was now running from my tears but I didn't
really care.

I picked up the bankbook. Inside was my name and a
balance of forty-eight thousand dollars.

I laughed through my tears. "Guess you borrowed a little
more than a smidge."

I must have been there for some time before calling black-
suit lady to come get me. The day had darkened.

"I hope we'll see you again soon," she said oh so insincerely.

I didn't have the strength for any bitchy comment at the
moment. Just when I thought there was nothing left to reveal,
nothing more to cry over, another layer rawer than the last came
up to rear its ugly head. I didn't know what was even holding me
together anymore.

Angus was waiting at home when I got there. He was sitting
at the kitchen table with Jude's purse in front of him. He seemed
startled when I started talking to him.

"Do you want some dinner?"

He just shook his head.

"Yeah. Me neither. I'm gonna go to bed." I put my hand on
his shoulder. His hand went over top of mine and he squeezed it.
I just about started crying again.

"You go on then and get some sleep," he said.

The next morning I woke up to see my phone blinking on
the nightstand. My heart skipped a beat as I realized that only
one person had ever left me a message on this phone. Much to
my disappointment, it was not Robert.

It was my ex-boss. And not just one message, oh no. That douche had to leave me five messages. Thankfully my cell phone didn't require me to listen to the whole message before I could delete it.

Emily! This is very unprofessional...deleted.
Emily, we can't find the contrast stain...deleted.
We found the contrast stain, but still call...deleted.
Look, I realize I was a bit hard on you. I'm...deleted.
I would like to renegotiate your pay...deleted.

I couldn't help but smile at the last one. Having no life since Julia passed away meant that I hadn't spent anything close to what I had made. I could have easily lived off those savings for a while, but then Jude had made bumming around even easier.

I stumbled out into the kitchen and saw Angus sitting there with a newspaper and two to-go coffees and what I guessed were a couple of pastries or something greasing up a paper bag.

"Hey Em!" he said brightly. "I was up pretty early so I went and got us some coffees. Jude showed me this coffee place and I have to say that, even though it costs you an arm and a leg, it is something else."

I held up my cup and saw that it was from *Starbucks*. Right, Angus had been dead long before this happened to North America.

I took a sip of my coffee, expecting the bitter bite of black java, but instead it was smooth and creamy.

"You got lattes? I would have never pinned you for a latte man."

Angus chuckled and took a drink of his. "Well you'd be right. I'm surely not a latte man." He said it just so, *LAH-tay.* "But your aunt gave me some pretty specific instructions before she left. First was that you like them lattes."

I nearly choked. "What? How the hell she'd know that?"

Angus shrugged. "Said you used to put so much milk in your coffee when you still drank it at home. Guess she just put two and two together."

I felt my throat tighten up in that all-too familiar sensation. "Didn't realize she was paying so much attention."

The cowboy laughed. "It's not like she was charitable about it. Said you liked your milk and not to say otherwise no matter how fat you got because you'd already had your share of misery. She said, If that girl wants coffee and milk, then Angus you get her coffee and milk or I will come back to haunt your sorry ass."

I started laughing. "Yep. That's my aunt, always watching out for my ever expanding rear."

A few lingering laughs trickled out in honour of my dead aunt before we both grew quiet again. It was a whole five minutes before either of us said a thing.

"Your aunt also left me instructions about what she wanted done with her remains." His voice had a question in it. *Do you want to hear this?*

I nodded. "Alright, what'd she want? Get sprinkled across the bingo hall's lawn?"

Angus smiled. "No. Believe it or not, your aunt was a romantic lady. She wants to be freed at the ocean, her words. But not just any ocean. She wants to be let out on the Californian coast."

"Like, send her off to sea?"

Angus nodded.

"Burned first, right? I think the whole body thing might be illegal." I suddenly pictured a group of small children at the beach poking my dead aunt's body with sticks after she'd washed up for a break from her eternal sail. Guess we could tie a sign around her saying *Please just give me a quick shove back into the water and I'll be on my way.*

"Oh of course, Em! Your aunt was only half crazy."

I held up my hands. "Just asking! Okay, so when is she getting cremated?"

"This afternoon. She had all the plans in place, so she is taken care of. We just need to pick her up some time tomorrow."

"Well, that works out well. I have no job, and we have no clue what the fuck to do with you, so...feel like going on a road trip?"

149

"I surely do. You'll have to rent the car though. Your aunt left money for that too, but I ain't got no license."

"Fuck it, let's go buy one."

1962 Olds

I had heard Angus coughing up a lung later that morning. It sounded like he was dying. I decided to let him pick the car.

He chose a 1962 Oldsmobile 98 convertible. We must have been at the dealers for close to three hours. Angus drove the car, then haggled. Checked under the hood, then haggled. Drove it again, then haggled some more. He got the car down from eleven thousand to thirty-five hundred.

"How'd you manage that?"

Angus shrugged. "This is a beautiful car but it runs like shit. That asshole was trying to pawn it off on some poor sucker just because it has some shiny paint and he managed to get the top working. It's alright though, I'll work on it for a bit tonight and by tomorrow it'll be good to go."

"I don't have any tools."

Angus stopped and thought about that for a minute. "Ah, don't worry about it. Look, I'm gonna drop you at home and get this bucket taken care of, alright? I might be home late."

I didn't see him again until the next morning.

"Hey Em! That car is gonna run like a champ!"

I shuffled over to the kitchen table and sat down to another morning latte and pastry. It was kind of nice having breakfast waiting for me. I wouldn't have eaten otherwise.

"Where'd you get the tools from?" I asked.

"Oh hell, I just borrowed them."

"From who? You don't know anyone around here, do you?"

"No, no. There's this garage just over on 4th. I talked to the owner for a bit about the car, and he let me borrow the tools."

"Aren't those, like, really expensive?"

He nodded. "I'm sure they are, but he was an alright guy. Just told him I was from out of town, just bought this for my niece and realized it needed a bit of work. Took him out for some beers afterwards, sorry I got home so late."

Just then, Mr. Puggums sauntered, and I mean sauntered, into the kitchen. He let out an ungodly mew and whole-heartedly ran himself along Angus's calf.

"Shit! I totally forgot about him! What are we gonna do with him?"

Angus looked at me like I was stupid. "What'd ya mean? He's coming!"

"What? You can't bring a cat on a road trip, they hate cars. Besides, he is freakin' old!"

Angus bent down and patted the old cat on the head a few times. The cowboy being sweet to a cat was a strange sight but so endearing.

"Nope, he's coming. It's his owner we're sending out. He should be there for that."

Just the way Angus said it...that's *that*. A fleshed out spook, a cat on the thin side of its ninth life, and me. What a crew.

"Is there anything else I can do for you today, Ms. Cameron?"

I shook my head. "No, this is good. Thanks."

I tucked the hundreds of American dollars away, stowed my new debit card and smiled at the nice lady at the counter.

As I turned around from the teller, I noticed a very tall man walking towards me. He was in his fifties but a good, healthy fifties.

"Ms. Cameron, how do you do?" he said as he stretched a hand out to me.

I must have looked at it like it was a used tissue.

"Pardon me, I'm Mr. Wilson. I've worked with your family for some time now."

I nodded and reluctantly took his hand. "Hi."

"I wanted to say I'm sorry to hear about Judith. She was a lovely woman."

"Yeah, thanks."

"Please pass my condolences on to Julia as well."

I hadn't been expecting that. "Excuse me?"

He looked confused. "Your sister, Julia?"

"How do you know Julia?"

"Well, uh...like I said, I've worked with your family for years."

I nodded. "Really? Well, if we were such important clientele, you'd be aware of the fact that Julia has been dead for three years. Have a good day."

I rushed past him and out the door of *Westpoint.* I knew it wasn't his fault for not knowing but I couldn't rationalize the anger I felt. When Julia died, my life had been blown into a thousand little pieces. The thought of someone not having even noticed her passing was almost too much to handle.

Road Trip

Huntsville is about an hour and a half from the border. With Angus at the wheel, it took us forty-five minutes to get there.

Angus didn't have any of the necessary papers to legally cross into the US. To be fair, he didn't really have any papers. And neither did Mr. Puggums. They'd both be walking out of Canada.

"Alright now, you're gonna hit the five as soon as you cross the border. Keep going and before you know it you're gonna pass through this spit of a town called Blaine. Have yourself a little picnic at the harbour." He hoisted Mr. Puggums out of the car. "We'll come find ya. And I won't be upset if you have a ham sandwich waiting on me."

He turned, stopped suddenly and came back to the car. "You might want to put your aunt in your purse. You never know what kind of prick you're gonna run into at the border check."

I have no doubt that most of Jude was still at the crematorium. I'd heard that the bones never burnt well but the families usually didn't want them. Maybe in another life I'd look down at such families, but right now I was really happy that the chunky, recognizably-human parts of my aunt were not here. Instead, what we did have of her was in a salsa jar. The urn the crematorium had given us didn't close properly. With so much driving ahead of us, we couldn't risk her spilling. I tucked her into the bottom of my bag and had my passport ready to go.

The border guard was fat and balding. He waddled as he walked around my car, trying on his meanest-don't-fuck-with-America face, but honestly, I had to keep myself from laughing.

His face reminded me of when Julia was five and had asked our mother why the old man was wearing his butt on his face. I'm not even kidding, my sister was perfect even then.

This guy was definitely wearing his ass on his face.

What's your business?

How long are you coming down here?

Do you know anyone down here?

What do you do? For how long?

I swear, he just about asked me when I last took a shit. Finally, he handed my passport back and sent me on my way with a look I know he was hoping instilled terror. It just looked like he was clenching his butt face really hard.

Sure enough, as the sun began to touch down for the day, a cowboy and his cat came to join me at the Blaine Harbour. It wasn't that it was far to walk, but the guards were intense and probably wouldn't have thought twice about shooting Angus.

I handed him a black forest ham sandwich as he settled in beside me.

"I guess we should hurry the hell up, eh?"

Angus took a bite and nodded. "Let's give this sunset a few more minutes. I made some bad choices when I was here the first time around but I always appreciated a good sunset."

Seabirds cawed and the ocean's saltiness was in every breath. I wasn't living the best life either but from then on I knew I wouldn't waste another sunset.

California

I'd been to California when I was a kid, before Julia was born. My mom came home from work and told me that we were going to Disneyland.

I was nine at the time. Thinking back on it, I'm pretty sure that's the day she'd found out she was pregnant because there were a lot of vomit stops along the three day drive to Los Angeles.

She couldn't go on most of the rides with me once we got there but she found sweet families in line-ups for me to pair with. All she had to say to the mom of the family was that she was in no condition to take me on the rides myself, and then she'd touch her belly. Yep, definitely preggers.

She always found me nice families though so I didn't mind. It was a great day.

Angus didn't need vomit stops, but he did have a few hacking fits along the drive that required us to pull over and wait it out. I offered to drive but he'd always wave me off, saying that he'd be fine in a minute.

And he always was, but more than once I saw him wipe a drip of blood from his lips. Whatever had gotten him the first time was just waiting to drag him down again. Every coughing fit was like a bloody note reminding him to pay up.

But not yet.

We made it to the Californian coast in less than two days. I don't know how he did it. The first thing we did was take my aunt Jude to the beach. I had a leash for Mr. Puggums. I know he hated it but it was better than taking him out in his crate everywhere.

The day was ending and the sunset was something to see.

"Do you want to say something?" Angus asked.

I nodded. I hadn't thought about it at all but it was just Angus, the cat and my aunt's roasted bones.

"I hope you had fun with my dead mother's money. I miss you."

I felt Angus looking at me. "Is that it?"

"She knows what I'm trying to say." I said. I wiped away some tears that had snuck up on me.

"Well, Ms. Jude. You made this old man's second round worth the wait. I'll miss you. Hopefully once I get up there you won't be too busy with your other boyfriends to see me for a trip to *Starbucks*."

I smiled. It was really sweet and strange hearing the cowboy make afterlife plans for coffee to a salsa jar full of ashes.

"Did you want to let her go?" I asked. "I don't mind."

He shook his head and handed the jar to me. "You go on. She stayed around as long as she did for you. You need to be the one to call it a day." He took his smokes from his rolled up T-shirt sleeve and lit up.

Instantly I pictured myself throwing the ashes against the wind leading to myself and Angus inhaling bits of Jude. Thankfully I checked the wind's direction after this thought. I thought about doing a test pinch just to make sure but that seemed really inappropriate for some reason.

I flung her up and away. Her ashes took on a new life and sailed out to the sea. It was the best of the three funerals I had been to.

"I think you and the other three spooks at the hospital proved that a body isn't what counts in the afterlife. Where do you think she's gone?"

Angus shook his head. "I have no idea."

We took in the setting sun at nearby picnic table. The air was warm and salty.

"I was never a church going kind of man."

"Angus, was that supposed to surprise me?"

He smiled. "That smartass tongue of yours is gonna get you in trouble."

157

"Until then gramps, continue on with your point."

"I was just thinking that even though I stopped going to church as soon as my mama realized that the devil had already claimed me, I still believed for a long time about heaven and hell. I thought for sure I was going to hell and that all those churchgoing folk were going up to the pearly gates. Once I got a mind of my own though, I started thinking that living bad Monday through Saturday and praying on Sunday probably wouldn't cut it. Even though I was no good Christian, I still kind of thought there was something to it. Thought for sure I'd end up in hell."

"Instead you got twenty to life in purgatory. Now you're out on bail."

He laughed. "Maybe that's just it. I slipped through the cracks so one of God's angels just stuffed me aside and hoped no one would notice."

"Sure, but what about the other three?"

He shook his head. "They're gone. I know that. Why I stayed behind, I have no idea."

"Maybe you're the angel. Sent down to give my aunt a good time before she kicked the bucket."

Angus chuckled. "Well, if that's the case then God is good to his angels."

We crashed at a *Motel 6*. I ordered us some pizza and we lazed about the room, watching *Friends* reruns.

"Oh and this is great, see, in later episodes they start dating but right now they're pussyfooting around one another like a couple of idiots." Angus explained.

I didn't have the heart to tell him that I, and every other twenty-six year old, had probably seen every episode of *Friends* at least twice.

"I wouldn't have pegged you for a fan of this show."

"Your aunt got me watching it."

Wow. *Friends. Starbucks.* What had my aunt done to the cowboy?

"So, what are we gonna do now?"

Angus sighed. Mr. Puggums creaked. My stomach made some interesting acoustic contributions.

"You know, Dolly used to talk about Las Vegas all the time. Like it was the bee's knees."

"She actually said it was the bee's knees, didn't she?"

Angus smiled. "Oh, probably. All the same, sounded like a place I would've liked to have seen."

Angus turned over on to his side to face me. "What'd ya think, Em? You ain't got no job. God only knows what kind of time I've got left. Feel like a drive?"

I nodded. "Las Vegas it is."

Las Vegas

We left the next morning. Los Angeles is two-hundred and sixty-five miles of road away from Las Vegas. This is nearly four-hundred and twenty-seven kilometres. At a reasonable speed of one-hundred kilometres an hour, this should have taken us at least four hours. Angus did it in three. I have no idea how. Maybe this whole ghost-now-trapped-in-my-old-failing-body was just a rouse. He might have actually been some kind of alien, able to bend the space-time continuum.

I had fallen asleep to a *Star Trek: The Next Generation* marathon the night before. No, Angus was probably just your run-of-the-mill spook...that was now in the flesh. If he could bend the space-time continuum, he probably would have done something much more impressive than shave an hour off our drive to Las Vegas.

We were there by noon. Angus and I had both been keen to stay on the strip but it turns out that pets weren't that welcome. We thought about sneaking Mr. Puggums in, but he wouldn't shut up for some reason. We ended up a mile from the strip in a *Comfort Inn*.

The cat calmed down once he had a bed to hide under.

"Alright, let's head out." Angus had just set our bags down and was already at the door.

"Yeah, alright. Let me just change."

Angus sighed. "You look fine!"

I was in an oversized T-shirt and fat-ass sweat pants. Yes, I'm sure I looked great.

"I'll be fifteen minutes, tops."

If I didn't know any better, I would have said that the cowboy was pouting.

Fourteen minutes later I was ready to go.

"See? That wasn't so bad. And now you don't have to be embarrassed to walk around with me," I said.

Angus's pouting face cracked a smile as we were heading out. It was only a mile to the strip, but this was the desert and Angus was old. We took the car and paid an outrageous amount to park it on the strip.

It was hopping. People milled about like ants in a frenzy over some dropped lollipop. Most people were easily passed, just like me and Angus. But some you just had to stop and have another look at. Double-D sized breasts dotted the crowd. Mile high purple hair on old ladies dressed in some kind of animal print poked through the throngs of people. The energy was palpable.

We settled on a buffet that just wouldn't quit. We gorged, moaned, waited it out and then gorged again. But the staff didn't care.

"I can't believe we just ate all that."

Angus patted his stomach and lit up a smoke.

"That Dolly, I could see her here in a heartbeat."

I laughed. "Yeah. I wonder what it looked like when she was here."

Angus took a drag and then eased out the smoke like one cool cowboy. "You never did tell me what happened to her."

I shrugged. "Do you really want to know?"

Angus seemed to be chewing on my question. "Sure I do," he finally said.

I sat up a little straighter. "Well, I wasn't having any luck with her name just popping up so I called everyone Dolly could remember. I finally got a hold of this bartender she used to know, Tula. Said that on Dolly's last night at Big Jimmie's, the club she used to work at, the boss set her up with a private party for some cops. She was never seen again."

"So she never made it to the *Rivera* stage, did she?"

I shook my head. "No. She had the costume because she was being fitted for it. Tula knows that the cops did something.

When she tried to tell them where Dolly had last been seen alive she got nothing besides having her windshield smashed in."

Angus was quiet for a long time after that. I just kept taking the complimentary Mai Tais the server was bringing me. I had polished off my fourth by the time Angus came to.

"That ain't right."

I snapped my head up. "What?"

"What happened to Dolly. It ain't right."

My head was swimming. Although the thoughts were there, they needed to be pushed beside one another before they made enough sense to be spoken aloud.

"No. It wasn't."

"Em, are you drunk?"

I looked at the cowboy and lined up a response. I pinched the air, to say *oh, just a little.*

"Come on. Let's get you back to the room."

I stumbled to our car. The short drive to our hotel was refreshing. Angus dragged me upstairs and got me settled in. He'd been asking me questions the whole way, none of which I remember answering.

Later that night I realized I must have answered some of his questions, and someone else had answered the rest.

When I woke, there was a fat, balding man tied up on our floor.

The Avengers of Moira Natalie

He had a goose-egg the size of a golf-ball just above his left eye. His right eye was boasting a shiner and his bottom lip was fat and purple. He was out cold.

Just then, Angus came from the bathroom. He looked at the prisoner, then saw that I was up. His face took on a hint of shame.

"Oh...Em. Sorry about this. Didn't mean to wake you."

"Who the fuck is that?"

"Oh, uh...well. Look it, there's no reason for you to be getting involved in all this, alright? Just go on back to bed. I picked you up some tomato juice and aspirin."

I was about to ask for what and then my head filled in the blanks. I jumped out of bed and ran for the bathroom. I couldn't have been asleep long because my vomit was speckled with bits of maraschino cherries from the one-too-many MaiTais.

"Oh, fuck my life," I shuddered. After I rinsed my mouth out, I filled up a cup from the tap and searched for the aspirin Angus had promised.

"It's the sugar. That'll get you every time."

I just looked at him as I popped back two pills. "Like I said. Who the fuck is that?"

I don't know if Angus thought that by reminding me I was hungover I would magically forget that there was an unconscious man bound by rope in our room. It kind of seemed like that's exactly what he had been hoping for.

"I dropped you off last night and went looking for that Tula Bing lady you told me about."

This memory was a wash. I decided that arguing the point wasn't worth the pain it would cause, so I just waited it out.

"Well, I found her and then we had a good chat about Dolly and such, and she gave me some names of officers that had been at the party with Dolly. Looked up a few and this was the first asshole I found alive." he said as he kicked the man's foot.

"Alright. But did you find him like that? All bruised and bundled up, ready to go?"

"Oh no, 'course not. He was having dinner so I waited for him. I told him I just wanted to ask some questions, but once Dolly's name came up he got all pissy and threatened to kick the crap out of me. Just didn't have the energy to duke it out with him. Guess I'm not the man I used to be. Just a swift tap to the head with a tire iron instead." There was regret in Angus's voice.

"So then you roped him up and brought him back here?"

Angus thought this over and nodded. "Yep, that's about what happened. And this fucker is gonna sing. Dolly's not gonna be some piece of trash they threw out. Not anymore."

We named him Fat Fuck. I suggested Fat Fred, but it turns out Angus used to have a dog named Fred and sharing that namesake with this guy was not an option.

Fat Fuck woke at around three in the morning. He was a little disorientated until Angus threw a bucket of ice water on him.

"Alright you sonovabitch. Where is she?"

"Look, I don't know!" Fat Fuck's voice was kind of whiny.

"Well ain't that just shitty for you." Angus sounded like a snake. The coolness of his voice made me shudder. Fat Fuck was not getting out of this one.

It took until seven-thirty in the morning before the cop was finally ready to talk. I have no idea where he'd gotten it, but Angus had a video camera set up and ready to record the cop's confession.

"My name is Lieutenant Herb Cooper."

Angus was looking through the man's wallet and nodded for him to continue.

"I've been part of the Las Vegas police force since 1972. In 1978, we had a retirement party for Captain Micheal Reich. We hired a dancer to entertain. Things got out of hand and she got hurt." He stopped and started sobbing.

Angus didn't say a word. It had been made perfectly clear to Fat Fuck what was required of him.

"We dumped her body two miles outside of town."

Angus turned off the camera and told me to pack up. We were checking out.

An hour later we were digging away at the second plot. Fat Fuck insisted that it wasn't a deep grave and we should have found her by about three feet. Angus had set up the camera on the tripod to watch the dig site and carefully directed me on where to dig so I stayed out of the shot.

After twenty minutes on the second plot, I brought up a shovelful of dirt with something shiny in it. Blue and red sequins. I dropped my shovel, turned around and barfed.

Angus came over and patted me on the back. I could hear him moving some more dirt around and then he sighed heavily. We had both known she was dead. But like this? Dolly, all by herself, spending night after night in the lonely desert.

Angus stabbed the shovel into the dry dirt and tied a red handkerchief to the handle. "Come on. Let's dump off this trash and be on our way."

We left Fat Fuck bound and bruised in front of the hospital with a note regarding the whereabouts of some remains and a video. The note requested that someone watch the video before handing it over to the police.

We headed straight out of town, not having played one nickel.

I don't remember falling asleep. I just remember waking up because the car lurched to a stop and Angus jumped out of the driver's seat and started hacking.

I groggily got out and went around the front of the car. We were on a completely empty highway in the early evening. Angus was spitting up gobs of bloody mucous. He heaved a few times and breathed as deeply as his rotten lungs would let him.

"Get in, I'll drive."

Angus just shook his head. "Nah, I'm alright. Sign back there said there's a motel coming up soon. We can stop there," he said, motioning to the empty road behind us.

I nodded. "Alright, let's go."

Thankfully, the motel came up in only another twenty minutes of highway. In fact, a whole town came up but both of us were too worn out to care.

"I'll get us a room. Be right back."

I could see that Angus was about to protest, saying he'd get the room, but instead he just nodded and slumped back in the driver's seat. He was so tired.

The Juniper Inn was old and smelled like it, but the room was clean. I couldn't complain.

Angus lay down and was out in two seconds. I left him a glass of water and went out in search of a gas station to buy Mr. Puggums a can of cat food. Poor thing had been living off of hamburger scraps since we'd sent off Jude with the wind.

There was a small gas station across the street that looked open. I grabbed a couple cans of pop, or should I say *soda* pop, chips, a package of *Ring Dings*, and then I cleaned them out of tinned cat food.

The guy at the counter had a grimy baseball cap on and looked like he hadn't seen a razor in about a week. His shirt had easily visible pit stains on it. He looked at me like I had three heads.

When I got back to the hotel, I realized why. My eyes were bloodshot, I had dirt smeared across my face, my clothes were still dusty from the digging that morning and my hair was a complete disaster. He had probably been afraid that I couldn't pay.

Mr. Puggums ate up the canned food like a *Hoover*. I left him to it and showered. The water was so warm and calming. I didn't know when the hysteria was going to hit. I'd dug up a woman that'd been dead for thirty years. We left a cop bruised and battered at a hospital with a video of his confession. Angus was real. Dolly had been real. I was not insane but everything else about my life was.

The towels felt like soft hugs. I don't know how long I stood there, holding the fluffy towel around me. This place might have been a dump, but it had great towels.

I crawled into bed and fell asleep to the sound of Angus struggling to breath.

I woke up to the rustling of a bag of chips. It was two in the morning. Angus was getting a snack.

"Hey, sorry Em. Thanks for picking this up." he whispered.

"Why are you whispering? I'm clearly awake now."

The cowboy laughed and sat down. "Sure, sure. *Ring Ding?*"

I sat up and took one. It tasted really good on my sawdust dry mouth.

He turned the night-table light on and flicked the television to life. *Sleepless in Seattle* was playing. I didn't ask him to change it and he didn't bother. We watched the whole thing except for the first fifteen minutes. By the end, we'd downed both cans of pop and one and a half bags of chips. Mr. Puggums was on his second tin of food.

"That movie..." Angus started.

"What?" I said.

"Ah nothing. Must have been to Seattle or something."

"Nice city." I wasn't sure if I should ask the question that was worming its way through my mind. Mostly because I wasn't sure I would like the answer. "Angus, do you think the cops will come after us?"

Angus shrugged. "They might. Can't see what good it'd do them. Tula's got a copy of the tape and she's going to show it to her niece or something or other. Says that this kid's into journalism or something. Besides, we're in Idaho now."

I sat up a little straighter. "Really? Where?"

"Twin Falls."

I couldn't believe that I had no idea where I was. This was the first time I'd thought about it. "Wait, I thought you left the tape with him."

Angus shook his head. "I made the bastard say his confession a few times. The official one with the dig site and all got mailed to Tula while you were rinsing your mouth out. I don't trust anyone else with it."

I nodded. "That was pretty fucked up."

"Yeah, sure was. Can't believe it took that long for someone to find her."

I knew Dolly wasn't waiting on anybody, but it was still good to know that this time at least one villain got a right good kick in the ass.

I woke up again at six to the sound of Angus hacking away in the bathroom. The people in the next room banged on the wall and yelled at us to shut up. I just yelled back, telling them to go fuck someone and to come over if they wanted a foot up their ass. I can't insult anyone worth shit at six in the morning, but they did stop banging.

I knocked on the bathroom door and gently pushed it open. Angus was leaning over the sink. It was covered with bright red splotches.

"I'm done Em," he gasped. "But I know where I need to get to."

"Where?"

"God love him, Tom Hanks and that blond girlie. I need to get to Seattle."

Seattle

We were in Seattle by five that evening. Angus had driven half way, but on the third pit stop I'd forced him into the back seat with a litre of water and a blanket. Mr. Puggums rode shotgun.

After we passed the Seattle city limit sign, I pulled over.

"Angus, we're here. Where to?"

He swallowed hard. "There's a hospital."

"There are probably lots of hospitals."

"It's funny looking. Like a school."

I noticed a man and a woman holding hands, walking along the side walk.

"Excuse me! Excuse me!"

They looked terrified.

"Sorry, but I'm not from here."

The woman took another step back. "We don't have any spare change!"

"What? No, I don't want your fucking money! Is there a hospital nearby, maybe a university hospital?"

The woman looked sheepishly at her feet. The man visibly relaxed.

"Yeah, you probably want the University of Washington's Medical Center."

"Any idea how to drive there?"

"Get back on the five, turn onto the 520. It's a whole mess of intersecting freeways. Then you'll cross the water on Montlake Boulevard, turn on Pacific. There'll be a bunch of signs and stuff pointing out the medical center. It's a bit of a ways."

"Yeah, thanks." I jumped back in the car and took one last look at the couple. The woman was shaking her head and looking generally humiliated.

As we crossed over a narrow water way between two bays, Angus sat up.

"Yeah, yeah. This is it. This is the way. I had fucking lung cancer."

"What?"

"I remember this, Em. I remember what happened to me!"

As we neared the medical center, Angus's excitement grew.

"That's where I kicked the bucket, watching the game." He smiled to himself, as if he'd figured out who dunnit before the show was even half over. "I can see it all now, Em. Keep going, no need to stop there."

I passed the turn off to the hospital and continued on.

"They drove my dead ass along here. My daughter, she spared no expense. Oak casket, her boy in a new suit, he's wearing my Red Sox cap. Turn here, your next right."

I turned down a dark street and came up beside a gated cemetery.

"I'm here." He got out of the car and stumbled along a gravel walkway that wound itself amongst the graves. "This is it."

He started coughing and fell to his knees trying to regain his breath. I came up beside him and helped him to his feet.

"Angus, come on, let's go."

He looked at me. "Go? Why the hell would we go? I need to see this!"

I felt the sting of nearby tears. "Why? So what if you're here? Come on, let's just forget about it. You need to go to a hospital!"

He shook his head and started stumbling forward again. I came up on his left and wrapped his arm across my shoulder. He smiled weakly at me.

"Just up ahead."

Each step brought me closer and closer to an edge. All I had was Angus and soon I was going to be alone. I could feel it.

We hadn't walked a minute when he stopped. To our right was a weathered headstone with Angus's name.

Loving father.

The cowboy slumped to his knees. He coughed up a mouthful of blood. I wiped away the trails it left on his chin with my hand.

"Now, Angus?"

I helped him rest up against his headstone. "Yeah, Em. Now."

My hand pushed away the tears that were now blurring my vision. "Fuck you, I drove your sorry ass all this way just so you could die on me? What am I supposed to do now?"

The cowboy smiled. "Stop chasing old men around and find yourself a young one."

"You can go to hell." I managed. It had no roar to it.

He just smiled again. "I might just be on my way."

"So this whole fucking time, you were a yankee cowboy from Seattle?"

His lips were red from the blood he was coughing up. "Yeah, I guess so."

I sniffed and wiped away a mess of tears and snot on my sleeve. "Explains the whole *Starbucks* thing."

"That coffee is something else." He coughed again and gasped for air in between fits. "Em, I want you to listen to me."

I nodded.

"Jude told me about Julia." He gasped and then swallowed before going on. "It wasn't your fault. Too many bad things caught her at the same time and that girl just couldn't do it this time around. You did right by her."

That was it. I started crying and couldn't stop. I don't know where Angus found the strength, but he managed to pull my head to his shoulder and wrapped his arm around me. It was finally done. I was completely naked now. My pain was on open display. As Angus's lungs bled out, my stone heart followed suit and broke into a thousand pieces, each dripping with anguish. I was done being hard, being cold and being alone. I grabbed a fistful of Angus's shirt and held on as if something like that could save me.

I don't know when my sobs quieted. All I remember is that as they did, Angus's breaths became shallower and shallower, until they finally stilled. He was gone again, but I couldn't move. Not yet. I fell asleep, resting my head on his shoulder.

I was sitting in a coffee shop across from Julia. She looked so beautiful. I tried to say something to her but my voice just didn't work. She smiled at me and reached for my hand. And then she laughed happily. It sounded like bells.

The morning light was just coming through the trees. I sat up slowly. My neck hurt so much. Guess using a tombstone as a pillow just doesn't cut it.

"Miss? Miss? Are you alright?"

A tall, spindly old man in a uniform was offering me his hand. I took it and he helped me to my feet. I was alone. Angus wasn't there, alive or dead. I must have had a strange look on my face.

"Uh, miss? Can I call someone for you?"

My attention snapped back to the old man. He was friendly looking in his shabby rent-a-cop uniform.

"No thanks. Sorry, I guess I fell asleep."

The guard smiled. "You wouldn't be the first. Come on, I'll walk you back to your car. I think your cat needs out for a minute."

"Oh shit!" I slapped a hand to my forehead. "Puggums!"

"Oh, I'm sure he's fine. The window's cracked for him."

Puggums was a wreck when I finally got to the car. I put the leash on him and let him wander around on the grass where he promptly took a crap.

"Uh...could you hold this?" I said, holding up the leash. The guard took it and I rummaged through the car for a bag. "Fuck!"

I came out and looked sheepishly at the guard. "Look, I'm really sorry. I don't have a bag."

Again, friendly smile. "You go on now. Snooker here will take care of it," he said, pointing a thumb to his chest.

I smiled. "Thanks."

"Sure thing. So you know the Starners?"

I shook my head. "No. Should I?"

He smiled. "The man's grave you were snoozing on. Mrs. Starner is his daughter. Comes once a month to see her dad. Must have been quite a guy to get that kind of devotion from a daughter."

My heart ached at the thought of Angus but there was some warmth there too. He had been loved and dearly missed.

I nodded. "Yeah, must've been."

Tunnel Ride Home

I don't remember the drive home. I don't even remember passing the border. Mr. Puggums must have been asleep when we did. Probably would have remembered being detained for trying to bring an animal across the border. I don't remember pulling up to my building and falling into my apartment. I don't remember any of it.

I just remember the questions that ran through my head. What was Angus? Had he been alive? Was I insane?

My phone was blinking when I got in. There was only one message and it had been sent the day after Angus and I had left. It was the boss.

Look, Emily. I know you don't think much of me as a boss. But I think a lot of you as a lab assistant. You're very valuable to us here. Even if you came back to train a new assistant, I would be very grateful. Take care.

"Well how do you like that?" I said to my empty apartment.

Mr. Puggums was kind enough not to leave me hanging and gave a right good screech in reply.

After a long shower I called my boss back and got his voicemail.

"Hey, this is Emily. I didn't call you back sooner because I was away for a funeral. I'm sure it's been long enough that you've figured it out but if you need any more help I'm happy to come by. And thanks...for your message. It was nice to get."

I got a call the next morning. The boss, who I was to now call Larry, asked me to come in as soon as possible.

Larry escorted me around the lab like a proud papa. He introduced me to people I'd worked with for the last three years as if it were Day One.

He had hired a new lab assistant. His name was Eric and he was a complete tool.

Larry left for a conference call and I sat with Eric and Lynn. I was trying hard to be kind but he was grating on me. Not because he had my old job. I just really didn't like him.

He was the kind of person that was told at a very impressionable age that he was smart. This is a bad thing because if said to a certain kind of person, they will feel no pressure to follow through with actually being smart. I've always believed that nine tenths of being smart was hard work. Eric had been smart enough to float through an undergraduate program, but too lazy to pull off the marks or work experience to go any further. He was all talk and this annoyed the shit out of me.

"Kirsing's methodology was elementary at best." Eric was turning his nose up at a recent publication from the lab situated one floor above us. I had read the Kirsing paper before I'd left. The methods were simple and absolutely brilliant.

"A child could have thought up that design," he continued.

I couldn't help myself. "And yet Kirsing was the first one to come up with it."

"Everyone's fawning over it like it's a stroke of genius!" he countered.

"Because it's simple doesn't make it stupid."

He shrugged. It was an arrogant shrug.

"Why don't you go eat your sour grapes somewhere else? Or better yet, why don't you get to work on that genius methodology you think so highly of. Wait, I know, I know! You can't because you are too busy shitting on the hard work and good ideas of people that actually contribute something worthwhile."

His nose twitched. He stood up and left.

As I went down in the elevator, I realized that I felt okay. Not elated, or even happy. But okay. I was going to be okay.

Even if the boss didn't end up keeping me on any longer than he needed to have Eric trained, it was going to be okay.

Eric. I was almost out the front doors of the building when I noticed him sitting alone in the first floor coffee shop. He looked really sad and kind of pathetic.

"Eric?"

He sat up straighter and tried to put on his best face but it was too late. I had already seen him looking like he was drinking steamed shit and there wasn't anything he could do about it.

"May I sit with you?"

He just shrugged.

I took a deep breath and sat down. "Look, I'm sorry if I embarrassed you earlier. I just have a lot of respect for Kirsing's work and I guess you caught me on a bad day." Lie. It was a good day. I just didn't like him.

He was looking off to the side when his nose crinkled up and his eyes started to fill with tears. Oh fuck, I'd made him cry.

"You're right though. I'm just jealous. I just...I went to school with Kirsing. Three years later I'm still bouncing around as a lab assistant and he's a lab's star student. It's like I just miss everything."

"Eric, he worked really hard to get where he is. Kirsing stays late, comes in early. There's a reason he's doing so well."

Eric nodded. "I know, I just...feel like I'm never going to get anywhere. I applied for grad school too, got it but just hated it!" He smiled but it wasn't a happy smile. "When I left my Master's project, I told my family it was because the lab head was a moron and wasn't challenging me enough. Truth was I had no idea what I was doing. It was painful going to the lab every day."

He may have been annoying but I still felt sorry for him. Nobody likes to have no idea what they're doing, especially when it seems like everyone else has it down. "Look, I don't know you but the first thing I got from you was that you think you're smart and you want everyone to know it."

He laughed weakly. "Don't hold back."

"I'm serious. Enough of an ego to have the confidence to try is one thing, but yours is a little much. And the sad thing is it isn't enough. Don't be worried to say I don't have a fucking clue. I bet if you had said that a few times during your Masters, someone would have helped you. You don't need to know everything or always one up everyone to make it."

"It's probably too late for me."

"Oh my God, you're not seventy. Talk to Larry, see if there are any projects he wants a student on. He's got a lot of grants coming in for work he can't do himself."

"Hence the grad students?"

I nodded. "You're learning from his experience, making some of it up as you go along and somewhere along the way you start to get some original thoughts. Then you write a paper like the Kirsing one."

He nodded. "Thanks Emily."

"Sure, see you tomorrow." I stood up to leave.

"Hey, Emily? Why aren't you a grad student?" He hadn't thrown it back in my face. It looked like he really wanted to know.

I smiled and shrugged. "Somebody's gotta keep the idiot grad students in line." That was all I could give him.

He laughed a little. "Okay. I'll see you tomorrow."

Julia's Guest

It was Saturday and I decided to do something I hadn't done in a very long time. Mr. Puggums screeched and hollered as I put my shoes on, so I just picked him up and brought him with me.

The cat was so used to car rides by then that I didn't have to put him in his crate anymore. He lay down on the seat beside me as we stopped at a market for some cheap but cheerful bouquets. We continued on to the cemetery where Julia and my mother were buried.

It was a nice day, with a clear blue sky. I put the cat on his leash, much to his chagrin.

For a second, I thought I had wandered into the wrong section of the graveyard. There was a tall man in a nice suit at my sister's grave.

I walked up slowly but he heard my footsteps and tried to straighten up.

I recognized him immediately. It was Mr. Wilson from the bank.

"Mr. Wilson? What are you doing here?"

He looked nervous for a second but then the exhaustion of grief overtook him. His shoulders slumped and his eyes sagged.

"Paying my respects. Nice to see you Emily." He turned and walked away from me.

I looked at Julia's grave. There were fresh pink daisies on it.

"Why?" I yelled after him.

He just kept walking. I picked up Mr. Puggums and ran after him. I caught up and gave a sharp pull on his arm that nearly made him fall over. He didn't yell at me or ask me what my problem was. He just took it.

"What are you doing here?"

Up close I could see that his eyes were old and tired and his slumped shoulders made his expensive suit and shoes look cheap. He was beaten in that moment, it was easy for me to recognize. "She was my daughter."

My mouth fell open as a question tried desperately to take shape.

"Your mother and I had an affair when she worked at the bank. When she told me she was pregnant, I...asked her to take care of it."

"Were you married?"

He nodded. "Yes, and still am. I panicked, but your mother was strong. She knew what was right for her."

"Did you fire her?"

He looked at me again and shook his head. "No. She quit. Said she wanted five thousand dollars for a new stroller, some baby clothes and so she could take her daughter on a trip to Disneyland."

My throat tightened but the words came out cold. "Yeah, thanks. It was a fun trip."

He smiled sadly. "I never had any other children."

"You didn't have any. Julia wasn't yours."

He looked confused for a moment. "But, I saw pictures of her, I..."

"If she'd been yours, you would have visited her on her fifth birthday with that fucking doll that talked and pissed itself. If she was yours, you would have taken her to the father-daughter dance when she turned ten. If she had been yours, you wouldn't have fucked it up this badly!" I was screaming with rage by that point.

He nodded. "You're right."

"For fucks sake, you didn't even know she was dead!"

"Your mother and I agreed that it would be best for her to not know who her father was."

"Well, you two were a couple of geniuses, weren't you?" My throat was tight. I was starting to cry. "If you had met her, just once, you would have known how great she was. You wouldn't have been able to forget about her."

179

"I never forgot about her."

"Well, she seemed to think so. Do you know how many times she asked about her daddy? Why she never heard from him, not even on her birthday?"

He bowed his head and his shoulders started jerking. He was crying too.

I turned away from him and went to sit down between my mother's and Julia's headstones. I pulled Mr. Puggums onto my lap.

"I was such a coward."

"Yeah, you were. She really could've used you in her life." I spit out each of the words.

He nodded. "I thought about her when I found out that you had come in for the safety deposit box. I thought, well, Judith the old bat is dead. And thankfully there's still something left for those girls. I wondered what she would do with the money. Go to Europe for a summer, buy a semester of random classes at a local college? Maybe a new car. But those hopes never had a chance, did they?"

"No. She was long gone."

"I used to dream about her."

"You didn't have to. You could have just visited her."

"I know." He didn't even try to fight off the guilt. He took it on as if the pain of it would somehow compete with the emptiness that I knew he was feeling.

And just then I pitied him. I had felt such guilt at Julia's passing. As much as I hated this man for abandoning my sister, I also understood the hollowness that he was feeling. And the fact that he felt anything said something.

"I've come here every day since you told me."

"How'd you know where to come?"

"I was here for your mother's funeral. It was the only time I saw Julia. I...I said hello to her and I remember for a second just thinking about picking her up and hugging her." He chuckled. "Your aunt shot me a look that could kill. I wish now that I had just done it anyways."

180

I laughed and wiped away my tears. "My aunt could be a real bitch sometimes."

He laughed and sat down across from me. "You remind me of your mother. She didn't take any crap from anybody. Probably why she stopped seeing me after she found out she was having Julia. She'd seen how spineless I was, probably realized there was no point in bothering with me anymore."

My mother had always been so patient and kind with me and Julia. It was frightening, hilarious and wonderful, all at the same time, imagining the kind of woman she was outside of being *mom*.

I laid out the two bouquets I had brought and stood up. Mr. Wilson stood up along with me.

"Emily, I know you don't think much of me and I know I don't deserve any better than that. But if you need anything, ever...well, let me know." He fumbled through his wallet and brought out a business card. He turned it over and wrote something down before handing it to me.

"There's my home number on the back. Anything, Emily. Anytime."

"Are you sure I should be calling your home number?"

He smiled sadly. "My wife knows everything."

I kept the snide remarks to myself about how she should leave his sorry ass. People needed each other for all sorts of reasons.

Leaving Home

Mr. Puggums greeted me at the door with a screech. I picked up the bony cat and carried him to the kitchen. After filling him up on some brownish chicken paste, we both sat on the couch and watched television. I had left a window open the entire time Angus and I were gone but the smell of smoke was still in everything.

It would be okay for a bit, but this place had too many ghosts in it. And that wasn't even including the actual ghost that had been here. I turned off the television, took a seat at the kitchen table and got out a pen and paper.

As I wrote a letter to my landlord, I realized that I had lived in this rental apartment since I was eight. Nineteen years later I was finally going to leave home.

My building manager had stopped by my apartment the day after I'd handed in my notice. "I wanted to say that I'm sorry to see you go. You and your aunt have been great tenants. No complaints about either of you!"

"Thank you." What was this lady's name?

"Well, say hi to Jude for me. Tell her to stop by."

"Uh...I'm really sorry you didn't find out sooner but my aunt passed away almost a month ago."

The little old lady's eyes got wide and frightened. "Oh my! I had no idea!"

"I'm really sorry. I didn't realize you two were friends." I suddenly felt really bad. I hadn't told anyone that she had died. I hadn't put it in the paper or called the bingo hall she frequented. I wasn't the only one that had known her, but it had never even crossed my mind that someone besides Angus and me would want to say goodbye.

She nodded. "Well, at my age you get used to this sort of thing. Still sad. She was a real nice lady."

"Yeah, she was really sweet."

"You know, I first met your aunt in the grocery store. This was a year after your mother had passed away. I was in line at the pharmacy to pay for my test strips and needles...I have the diabetes disease, dear. Anyways, I didn't have anywhere near enough and she helped me out. I was able to pay her back the next month, but that was still a kindness I never forgot. Where is she buried, dear? I wouldn't mind putting a few flowers down for her."

"Well, actually, she requested to be cremated and released on the Californian coast."

"Well, my! Now isn't that the way to do it!" You'd think I'd just told her that my aunt was taking a luxury cruise around the world the way she gushed about the final arrangements.

I nodded. "Yeah, guess my aunt was a bit of a closet romantic. Anyway, I'd better go or I'll be late for work. So out on the 30th by noon?"

The little old lady shrugged and smiled. "You just drop your keys off and a forwarding address whenever you're heading out. I'm not gonna cry if this place airs out for a couple of weeks."

That night I left the lab at six instead of five. George had a mouse experiment to do and wanted me to help. I had agreed on the condition that he didn't touch any of the animals.

On my way home I picked up a pineapple and cheese pizza, a grape slushie and a bag of five cent candies.

Tomorrow was Saturday. I had decided that that would be the day to clean out Julia's room, so tonight I was having all her favourites.

I had no idea where she was. Maybe she was living in the wall of an abandoned farmhouse, rattling chains in some old castle in Europe, or maybe she was wherever Angus and the others had gone on to. But she wasn't here. Each thing in her room was a memory of her that I had bottled up. For her sake and mine, I was ready to let go.

I had told myself that I would be able to keep one thing of hers and the rest would be given away. I ended up with two grocery bags full of stuff I was keeping, but I decided to not give myself any grief about it.

I had kept her teddy bear named Pig; a framed photograph of her and our mom; another one of her and me; her favourite t-shirt, which I told myself would only be okay if I actually wore it occasionally; her diary, which I would never read; her special Barbie doll collection that consisted of three dolls with mix and matched limbs secured with glue and cropped and marker-coloured hair; an unopened glass bottle of coke and her baby blanket. She had called it Hanky until she was six.

My aunt's room would be easier.

By Monday, my living room was full of bags and boxes of things to give away. There wasn't even standing room. I had booked the day off knowing the disaster that would await me, but this was worse than I had imagined. I had called Big Brothers that morning and they had agreed to stop by around noon as they would be in the area anyway. All I had to do was get my donations to the front lawn.

By the sixth bag I was swearing the whole way down. This building was full of seniors and to take up our only elevator for this would have ruffled some geriatric feathers. I was sweating and my hair was sticking to my face.

"Emily?"

My stomach dropped four feet and I felt the cold pizza I had had for breakfast rise up in my throat.

It was Robert.

I just looked at him.

"Hey. Are you having a garage sale?"

I didn't process his question and it must have shown on my face.

"I mean, you're putting all this stuff down here...I just..."

184

I finally shook my head. "No, no. I'm getting some stuff out here for Big Brothers to come pick up."

He nodded. "Heard you quit the lab."

"I heard the same thing about you."

"Yeah, well, I figured it was time to move on."

Like a girl, my brain tried to work out the numerous double meanings of everything he was saying.

"I'm sorry," I blurted out. "I'm so sorry for what I said to you. You're one of the best people I've ever known. I didn't mean any of it."

He did nothing for what felt like forever.

"Anyway, they're going to be here at noon so I gotta..." I didn't finish my sentence. I just started walking backwards.

"Em?"

I sucked in a breath of air. "What?"

"Would you like some help?"

I felt my face squish up in confusion. "Uh...sure. Yeah, if you've got time."

"I've got some time."

I ordered in Thai food and we sat on the front lawn of my building waiting for Big Brothers to show up. It was already three in the afternoon.

The day was warm but not hot. It was kind of perfect.

"How's Toronto?"

Robert smiled. "It's good. It's really good."

I nodded. "That's...good."

"Yeah. But I've decided to take a break. My supervisor is great though, so it wasn't a problem."

"Oh yeah? What are you gonna do?"

"I'm going to Europe."

"Seriously? That's...wow. When?"

He shrugged. "Came back to see my parents. Thought maybe I'd check in with a friend, see if she wanted to come with me."

"Oh." I looked down at the noodles I was eating.

He sighed. "I take it that's a no."

I dropped my food. "What? Me? You want me to go with you?"

He looked at me like I was very stupid. Probably because I was. "Yes you. Why do you think I'd have brought it up?"

"I don't know, I just...but I'm so mean! I can't even believe you're speaking to me right now, let alone asking me to go to Europe with you!"

He smiled and brushed away some hair from my face. "No, you weren't mean. You were just sad."

The cold part of me that had kept it all under wraps for so long wanted to ask him what his problem was, didn't he know punishment when it was repeatedly kicking him in the face. But that part of me was just a little too quiet then, so I kissed him instead.

Two Weeks Notice

I gave Larry two weeks notice this time. He appreciated it immensely and told me to come back any time.

It was my last day at the lab. Robert had also been coming in. He was helping to sort out a few pieces of his work for Larry. It was good research and it was nice to know it wouldn't be rotting away somewhere, becoming less and less relevant by the day.

"Emily?"

It was Lynn. "Yeah?"

"The boss wants to talk to you."

I nodded. "Sure, I'll be there in a second."

"He insisted. Right now."

I sighed. Since coming back to the lab I had realized that even though Larry, the boss, could be a complete tool, he was also smart and hadn't gotten to run his own lab by luck alone. He had just fallen into the trap of running it all and not doing anything anymore. It wasn't his fault research was such a rat race.

Even so, I hated being interrupted. I quickly finished the last staining step of my slides and put them aside.

"Alright." I went over to the sink and started to wash my hands. "Any idea what it's all about?"

She shook her head just a little too fast. It suddenly dawned on me that the lab was empty.

My stomach knotted as I followed her out of the lab and into the small conference room.

"Surprise!"

I smiled and nodded as graciously as I could. I hated surprises. I had had more than my fair share of them and I didn't want anymore. But this was really nice of them.

There were pink streamers twisted around the room. Clusters of pink balloons made me think *Barbie Hemmorrhoids*. Cups and napkins were the same hue of giggling pink.

"Wow, thank you guys. This is so nice of you."

Robert came over and hugged me.

"I'm so sorry," he whispered. "Larry insisted."

As he pulled away, my smile got even bigger. I couldn't help it. He made me really happy.

"Emily! Come look at the cake George made you!" Lynn said excitedly.

I moved around a few people to see a massive white lump on the table. It was a sleeping mouse about the size of a cat. It had wings made of cardboard and, in baby blue icing, *All lab mice go to heaven* was scrawled across it's rump.

"Oh my God, George. This is really good!"

He smiled as if to say *ah shucks*. "Wanted to bring something nice to your party."

"You made this?"

He nodded. "Yeah, well, you can't just read papers all the time. Gotta have a hobby. My sister got me into it."

"It's great. And just to show my appreciation, I'm even gonna let you cut me a piece."

George laughed. "Sure, sure."

As he hacked away at his cake, Larry came up and gently tugged my arm. "I just want you to know how valued you are here. I think back to that speech you wrote for me, you remember? On the work that Robert was doing?"

"Yeah, I think so."

He leaned in close and whispered like we were co-conspirators. "I didn't even read it until I was up there!"

I feigned surprise. "Oh really? That's not very...diligent."

He smiled sheepishly. "Oh I know, I know. But it was the best thing I've ever done. You know, people still send me emails about that little speech, saying how it reminded them of what it was like as a grad student and how they would try to be better bosses." He sighed. "After you left, the first time, I mean. Well, after that I realized that what you said, about appreciating those who do the work that we present, also applied to you. This lab ran because of you." He looked like he was going to cry. "As was clearly evidenced once you left, because for awhile we had no idea what was happening." He chuckled.

"Thanks. That really means a lot."

"If you need a letter or anything, you just ask."

Celebrating my departure had a certain irony to it. I had treated everyone here like vermin for several years. If I were them, I'd be celebrating my departure too. But I knew there was no anger here, despite my best efforts. Most people didn't care I was leaving, but a few would actually miss me. That was more than I could have hoped for.

We were leaving the next day. I had packed my bags, unpacked them and then packed them again. My passport, credit cards, reservation printouts and Tylenol were all safe in my carry-on bag. It was only six in the morning.

Maybe that was the problem. I was too excited to go. I was too prepared. Something had to come along to fuck it all up.

Stanley

The four hour drive up to Appletown went by in a blur. The call I received that morning had been pushed to the back of my mind as I set myself on auto-pilot to make the trip up here.

As I stepped out of the beast of a car Angus had left me with, I wondered if I had crashed into anyone or anything along the way. I wandered around the front of my car just to make sure. No dents, no scratches, no wildlife pinned fatally underneath.

My palms started to sweat and my breathing suddenly became difficult. I felt as though I was about to pass out. I leaned against the warm hood of my car and waited a moment. My breathing slowed, the spots disappeared, but the sweaty palms were there to stay.

Stanley was no longer in the psychiatric hospital. He was in Appleteown's general hospital, which was a small, compact, one-story affair. Like so many buildings on the coast it looked rundown from the drips of moss that dirtied up its exterior.

The receptionist directed me to the acute medical wing of the small hospital. It was to the left. That was how small the hospital was. If it's really bad, go left. If it's not so bad, go right.

The nurse greeted me warmly as she led me over to Stanley. I gasped as I finally realized which of the patients she was bringing me to, but she either didn't notice or was too polite to chid me for it.

Stanley's ear was bandaged, as was his left arm. His hair was sticking out in tufts amongst scabbed over bald spots. He turned to me and drunkenly smiled.

"Is he sedated?"

The nurse nodded. "Yes dear, absolutely."

"Why?"

"Well, it was either that or strap him down. I guess when you get right down to it, there's not much difference, but for him, this was the better choice. He lost some blood and hasn't been eating. His body needs time to rest up after what he did to himself."

I couldn't look at her. "Okay, thanks."

"Alright, now you just call if you or your dad needs anything."

I nodded and took a seat beside Stanley at the window.

That morning they told me he had had an incident that was quite serious. He had been put into an isolation room where he had pulled his hair out. He then pushed past the nurse when she came by at night to check on him. He broke a window trying to escape, cut his arm, and then grabbed a shard of glass and had worked a third of the way through his ear before he was wrestled to the ground. I remember hearing the obvious fear in the doctor's voice as he told me this.

I looked over at him again. He was still smiling as he looked out the window.

"Why'd you do this, Stanley?"

He looked at me slowly and shrugged.

I took his good hand and squeezed it. "You're a fucking mess, you know that, right?"

He smiled again and nodded slowly but deliberately.

"I'm sorry. For what happened to you. This sucks."

He nodded again. "It's...okay. I'm...okay."

I nodded and we both looked back out through the window. I stayed there until dinner time.

As I got up to leave him, he squeezed my hand affectionately. He still looked drunk, but his smile was sweet.

"You...were better off...without me," he said purposefully.

I felt my throat tighten. I couldn't say anything. Instead, I squeezed his hand in return and left.

As I slid into the front seat of my car, my whole body suddenly felt very heavy. It was an effort to get my bag open and check my phone.

There were seven missed calls, three voicemails and five text messages, all from Robert.

I didn't bother listening to any of the voicemails. I figured the variations on *Where are you?* that filled my text message inbox were probably reflective of the voicemails.

I lowered my seat back and felt my exhausted body relax. Maybe I was better off without Stanley around. Maybe he would have been unreliable, or maybe even terrifying.

I knew I was going to fall asleep but I didn't care. Robert would be on a plane to London the next morning, without me.

He was better off without me.

My dreams that night were incessant. Flashes of images bounced amongst short skits performed by the puppets in my mind, all of it having an unnamable flow to it, but being completely nonsensical at the same time.

Only one stuck with me in the early morning hours. I was walking up to a white table where Angus and Julia sat. They both had solemn looks on their faces.

As I took a seat at the table, Julia started yelling but I couldn't hear what she was saying. Angus started in too. I tried to get them to talk one at a time but there was no use. They wouldn't stop shouting until finally their calls began to synchronize and the words took on a lazy shape in my ears.

They were asking what the fuck my problem was.

I woke up with a start. I grabbed my cell phone and checked the time. It was three in the morning. The four hour drive back would put me in Huntsville at seven and then it would be another hour to the airport. I turned the key and the Oldsmobile roared to life. My flight was at nine-thirty.

I made the four hour trip back to Huntsville in three hours. The roads had been completely empty and dry. I pushed the speed limit by twenty kilometres an hour.

Huntsville was still asleep at six in the morning. I thought about stopping to pick up my bags and decided against it. Mr. Puggums was already with the landlady and, if she needed to, she could throw all my luggage away. I had my ticket and passport in my purse, it would be enough.

Robert had been forgiving of all my horrible treatment but I knew that this would be too much. He had a life to live and couldn't be worrying about the next time I would decide to call it quits and ruin everything.

I'm not sure why, but I hadn't thought to call him until then and the idea hit me as if I'd just conceived of the light bulb.

I was stopped at a red light at an empty intersection when I pulled out my phone and dialed Robert's number.

"Emily?" he nearly shouted. "Where the hell are you?"

"I'm on my way. I'm..." I had no idea what to say.

"Em? Are you still coming with me?" His voice was so much quieter now, as if he didn't dare push me too far.

"Robert, I can't promise you that I won't be a complete fuck up from time to time. I don't want to be such an asshole, especially to you, but I just..."

"Em. Please, are you coming?"

I breathed out slowly. The lights had changed twice already. "Yes, Robert. I'm on my way."

I heard him sigh. "I love you, Em. Call me when you get to the airport."

I pushed away the tears that had been gathering. "I love you too Robert."

I looked out the small window beside my coach seat. It was overcast today.

"Miss? Miss? Could you please put your purse under your seat?" the flight attendant asked urgently.

"Oh. Sorry," I said as I tucked away my bag.

Robert smiled at me. "You're being kind."

I shrugged. "Not her fault that her job equates to being annoying."

He laughed. He took my hand and squeezed. "I'm so happy you're here."

"You say that now. Wait until our passports get stolen or I drink too much and get detained. We'll see how much we like one another then."

"This is gonna be a great trip."

I nodded. "I know." Old habits were dying hard and I just about didn't say anything else. "I'm so glad you came back."

He leaned over and kissed me. "Me too. What can I say? I missed my psychopath."

I punched him in the arm. "What? Maybe sociopath, but psychopath?"

He laughed and grabbed by fists. "Okay! Okay! You win! Sociopath with a side of anger management issues."

I smiled as I sat back in my seat. The flight attendant looked at me.

"That bitch hates me."

"Who? The flight attendant?"

I nodded.

"Yeah, probably. But you hate her too."

"That's true."

We settled into our seats. Robert held my hand as the plane sped down the runway and lifted off the ground.

I knew this trip wouldn't change my life. That was up to me. But it still felt amazing to lift up and off the ground, as if I could outrun old pains, even just for a little while. I was happy.

Epilogue

After coming back from Europe, I made a one day stop in Huntsville to pick up Mr. Puggums and then I was on the next plane to Toronto.

For the next six months, I lived with Robert on the other side of Canada. I would still be there except Robert had a conference in Vancouver and had asked me to come with him.

I didn't stay for the conference.

I drove my rental car into Huntsville. I didn't stop until I was at the old forest. I had a flat of colourful flowers and a small shovel in the seat beside me.

Carrying the flowers down the worn path underneath the forest's canopy was treacherous. I nearly dumped everything twice.

The hospital was still there. Alone and pathetic. I didn't dare go inside.

I carried the flowers around back to where the old picnic table still stood. The garden beside it had rich earth and a healthy assortment of weeds.

I worked away at the soil for three hours, clearing away the weeds and turning over the dark brown dirt.

Finally, I was ready to plant.

I didn't space them out too much. I just kind of plotted the flowers wherever. I stood up and looked at my work. It was really pretty.

I was about to take a seat at the picnic table when something stopped me. Sitting there on the bench was an old, weathered red baseball cap. It was a Red Sox cap.

ABOUT THE AUTHOR

J.E. Flanagan lives in Vancouver, British Columbia with a hungry cat named Zac. She can be contacted at:

www.emilysseams.com

CPSIA information can be obtained at www.ICGtesting.com
Printed in the USA
LVOW132115100612

285494LV00009B/20/P